APOCALYPSE
ALL THE TIME

David S. Atkinson

Literary Wanderlust LLC | Denver

Published in the United States by Literary Wanderlust LLC, Denver, Colorado.

www.LiteraryWanderlust.com

Library of Congress Control Number:

ISBN print 978-1-942856-07-8

ISBN digital 978-1-942856-08-5

Cover design: Ruth M'Gonigle

Layout design: Meghan McLean

Printed in the United States of America

Dedication
For all those left behind on May 21, 2011.

Part I: That's Great, It Starts with an Earthquake

"What we've got here is failure to communicate. Some men you just can't reach. So you get what we had here last week, which is the way he wants it. Well, he gets it. I don't like it any more than you men."

-Captain, *Cool Hand Luke*

Frank: "28 days, 6 hours, 42 minutes, 12 seconds. That is when the world will end."

Donnie: "Why?"

-Donnie Darko

Chapter One

Someone ran into the room where Marshall had been sleeping. He'd been dreaming of being pursued by robed riders on skeletal horses. One person ran into the room, and then more people followed, their steps echoing everywhere. It got louder. He opened a tired eye, but he was alone in his apartment. The rumbling continued.

Then, the building was on log rollers, rumbling back and forth. Marshall was disoriented as he lay in bed. His body, always feeling a little oversized, seemed disconnected from up or down. Rudderless.

An earthquake.

Marshall tried to remember if they were still on Earth. So many things had happened and it was difficult to keep track of everything. If he was still on earth then it was only an earthquake. Otherwise, it'd be a something else quake.

Same difference for what it meant, but the distinction seemed as important as anything else. It was at least as important as the fact it was happening, which itself wasn't a big deal.

Marshall grabbed the side of the bed to pull himself out from under the blankets. He let his body roll onto the floor and tried to stand. Nothing fell off the walls, but only because Marshall had never bothered putting anything up. He started toward his front door.

It was just the apocalypse.

An earthquake apocalypse.

The ground under people's feet would betray them. Great cracks would open and swallow up men without thought, without intention. Buildings would crumble. People would die. Continents would shift. Life would change forever.

Marshall yawned. He rubbed sleep from his eyes. He ran a hand through his shaggy, black hair. Then he emerged from his apartment, sure his pale skin made him seem like a naked mole rat tentatively greeting the day.

Oh well.

In the hall, a flood of people screamed, and flowed toward the stairs, pulling Marshall awkwardly along with them. He couldn't be sure who was screaming. There were so many people everywhere. Nobody seemed to be yelling, but everybody seemed to be. It was disembodied screaming, and Marshall stopped thinking about it when he remembered he didn't care about who it was.

The flow swept him down the cement stairs. No one took the elevators during an emergency. They were well trained. The flow surged Marshall downward. Some people tumbled, but only onto other people. No big problem. No one seemed to be getting crushed. There was that at least.

The mass broke outside, each out for themselves, running anywhere away from the buildings.

The open.

The instinct was to head for the open.

Marshall found himself in a nearby green space. It was like a park, but with nothing in it. Like a vacant lot, but mowed. It was probably important for something, but for the moment, Marshall thought it best for avoiding earthquake dangers.

There was a tearing sort of roar. Marshall looked up to see an apartment building separating into halves. Like a wishbone, though Marshall didn't bother making a wish. Steel frames shrieked and twanged, snapped. Bricks crumbled to powder. The whole thing fell to the ground as if it was tired and needed to sit.

No people died though, apparently. It looked like everyone had gotten out. That was a nice thing.

Other buildings fell.

Then the shaking stopped. People looked around, Marshall along with them. Thousands of voices buzzed, probably trying to ask what was going on. Confusion. It all merged into a giant mass of noise-thought. Indistinguishable sound like listening to all the broadcast stations at once. No message remained in all the messages. Then the rumbling began again. Stronger.

A red-haired woman in a brown jumper grabbed Marshall. She pulled him down to her and jammed her tongue into his mouth, searching. Need.

Surprised, Marshall returned the rutting kiss.

The woman was short and curvy. The jumper stretched, emphasizing attractive bulges. Not that he'd had a chance to judge, but Marshall felt attracted. His instinct wasn't to push her off.

She ground her hips into him, something to which Marshall was unaccustomed. It wasn't like he'd never been with a girl before, only it was usually a lot more work. Meeting, expressing interest, pursuing, and mood setting. A choreographed and stylized dance. It was kind of refreshing to have one just show up.

Her hands groped at his belt. She moaned. "Come on. We don't have much time. This could be it."

Marshall froze, disgusted. His arousal drained. The redhead repulsed him. She smelled of saliva and sweat, though she'd smelled of sex a moment before. Her grinding now seemed like an attack, desperate. She clung like a maggot, a greasy, rotting maggot. The taste of bile rose in Marshall's throat.

The redhead didn't seem to notice, still humping Marshall's leg. Maybe she didn't care. She still pulled at his clothes, frantic. Drool leaked out one side of her mouth.

"Get me off. We're going to die."

Marshall broke away. Stunned, he didn't go far. He had to get the redhead off him, get her out of his face. He couldn't breathe.

The woman didn't pursue. She almost didn't pick up on his departure, instead grabbing a fat man nearby. She latched on and the fat man did the same.

"We're going to die," the woman shrieked as a crack tore through the green space, splitting earth, and knocking everyone off their feet. "Do it, now."

The redhead and fat man pulled at their clothes, frenzied. As soon as a path was open, she thrust herself onto him. The fat man grunted, red-faced, and pumped furiously. They looked like pigs.

Marshall stared in horror, wishing he could look away.

"Faster," the woman screamed, "before it's too late."

The fat man's flesh rolled. It jiggled and shook more than the world around them. The coarse hair on his hide was flecked with bits of white deodorant, and the scent of rotting milk wafted off of him. He groaned and squealed, frantically trying to finish. He barely seemed to notice the redhead.

Marshall finally broke his gaze, but turned to another nude, copulating pile, a mass of arms and legs groped and pressed. Women, men, old, young, beautiful, diseased. It didn't seem to matter. A hole, or not, completely willing, or not, living, or not. Piles of one, piles of many, piles merging into bigger piles. They were scattered everywhere.

Marshall backed away, as if the piles of humanity weren't fornicating in all directions. It wasn't really shocking, though it startled him at first. At least, it wasn't any more shocking than any of the other times it happened.

Not everyone rutted. Marshall saw someone sucking down cigarette after cigarette, and another sucked down multiple cigarettes at a time. One man chugged whiskey, brown rivulets running down his chin.

Last moments. The last thing people thought they'd be able to do.

A store window shattered. Pillage. It struck Marshall as odd there was anything to steal. People weren't even looking at what they were grabbing, they were just taking.

Marshall did nothing. No last cigarette. No last drink. No last orgasm. Not again.

He looked around at everyone. Didn't they remember the last time?

The quaking went on. The green space split open and Marshall left. He kept to wider streets, those bordered by shorter buildings, or buildings that had already fallen. Cabling dangled and whipped through the air, sparking. Water shot from snapped pipes. Marshall avoided it all calmly, disinterestedly, making for the limits of town.

Outside the city would be safest. It bored Marshall, but he wasn't going to let himself die. At the very least, he wasn't going to wait around and let it happen.

A few others were making for the edges of town. Their first reflex got them out of their homes. Then they partied. Or panicked. Partied seemed to be the wrong word. Their behavior was too desperate, too crazed. It was like a party in some ways, but there was no enjoyment in it.

Marshall had no joy, but no desperation either. It was just time to get to safety. The others could wallow all they wanted. Marshall couldn't understand why they wanted to though.

Then the sky blazed with light. It was the image of a man, elderly though not weak, on what looked like a throne backed by a room covered in deep blue velvet. Perfectly straight gray hair, facial hair, ordered in appearance. He wore stiff maroon long-coat and breeches, with spider-web cords, and a light shirt of woven silver, as usual. All this was an impossible number of feet high. The projection covered the sky from horizon to horizon. Again, as it usually did.

Malcolm.

Marshall had been wondering when the amelioration broadcast would start. It seemed like it had taken a while this time.

"Citizens," Malcolm's voice boomed from the sky. The people looked up from their piles. The bacchanalia halted.

Marshall wondered how they handled the audio portion of the broadcasts. The image was simply projected onto ever-present atmospheric moisture. There was no need for a receiver, no need to worry that anyone wouldn't be able to see. The audio though. Marshall wasn't sure how they managed the audio so everyone would be able to hear. He'd never thought to ask.

"Do not panic," the booming voice from the heavens continued. "Unknown geological processes at the core of the planet have rendered the surface unstable, creating a globe-wide series of seismic events. However, do not fear. The Apocalypse Amelioration Agency has the situation well in hand. We will save you all. There is no cause for alarm."

Marshall heard a nearby crowd exhale a collective sigh of relief, though he couldn't imagine why. The agency always fixed things. This wasn't a surprise. Marshall agreed with being cautious, but actually being worried struck him as being a tad melodramatic.

"Top scientists are currently devising a solution to stabilize the anomaly at the core. Our drills will reach the necessary depth shortly, and we have every reason to believe we will then be able to reverse the geothermic reaction. Salvation will not be long, now."

Marshall tuned out, and continued toward the outskirts of the city. The explanation was pointless though the others he passed were eating it up. Something was wrong. It would be fixed. Beyond that, the details weren't significant. It'd probably never happen again, in the same way at least, and Marshall wouldn't be the one to fix it if it did happen again. So why dwell on details?

"Until we restore stability, all citizens should remove themselves from developed areas. Gather in the cleared zones bordering your towns and cities. Agency personnel will be on hand to implement order and answer any questions. Rescue skiffers will collect anyone trapped or buried under debris and bring them to centralized recovery points. Please do not worry about relatives or other loved ones. All will be safe and will be reunited with you soon. Concentrate on your own safety for the moment."

Marshall doubted from what he had seen that anyone had been worried about friends or family. They hadn't stopped thinking of themselves long enough to consider anyone else. Still, perhaps they would have later.

Malcolm's image straightened. That usually signaled he was wrapping things up.

"Again, remain calm. The Apocalypse Amelioration Agency has your best interests in mind. The earth may end life as we know it, but we will march onward. We will adapt, we will begin anew. All will be well."

As usual, Malcolm smiled.

"Now, citizens, please proceed to those areas of safety. We all have much work to do."

The sky went dark or seemed to. The sun still shone, but the extra illumination of Malcolm's image had disappeared. They were all on their own again.

People didn't freak out again though. They collected themselves and began doing what Marshall had been doing all along—leaving town. It was different once they had directions. Even with Malcolm no longer directly over-head, his orders seemed a solace. Everything had changed.

Marshall shook his head. Of course, people should gather in the cleared zones. Those were obviously the safest places in an earthquake. And, of course, the agency would stop the quakes if possible. That's what they did. He just couldn't grasp what altered for people when Malcolm came out and said it.

Regardless, people were suddenly content. They chatted as they walked. The quake was still going on, but the tremors were weaker. They subsided and people in the crowd joked about them.

Marshall's mood darkened as everyone else's mood brightened. It wasn't the apocalypse. Marshall's feelings about that were pretty pragmatic. The crowd, however, depressed him. He wasn't quite certain why, and didn't particularly want to think about it. Whatever the reason, the people irritated him.

He almost wished they were still rioting and he alone was proceeding to safety. He was horrified at himself. Quickly, he rationalized he didn't want any of them harmed. It wasn't that at all. It was only he wished he didn't have to be around them all. He wanted to be alone.

Marshall shook his head again when he realized he was justifying his own thoughts to himself. Then he made an attempt to stop thinking so much and simply follow the crowd to the cleared zone.

After all, it was the apocalypse. Again.

Chapter Two

Even apocalypses got old after a while.

Marshall couldn't be sure exactly how many apocalypses there had been. He wasn't sure when the first one happened. He might not have been born then. They could have been going on for quite a while before, but he wasn't sure. It had certainly been a while, but quite was at least as long as he remembered.

That was one side effect of apocalypses, skewed time perception. An apocalypse tended to redefine time in terms of itself. When you had one or more a month, time lost a bit of meaning.

There was usually, at least, one a month. Sometimes there was more than one a week, or even two in the same day.

It might have been more than a month between the quakes and the previous apocalypse. Marshall wasn't certain. The last one had been the green fever plague.

At least, Marshall was pretty sure the green fever had been the apocalypse immediately prior. That was the last one he remembered. It was possible there was another in between which he'd forgotten. Heck, there could have even been one in the interim he hadn't noticed. That was always possible. He could have slept through one. Apocalypses may not have happened every day, but it wasn't far off to say they did.

He remembered the green fever plague apocalypse specifically because it was so badly named. It didn't turn people green, instead tending to turn them purplish, or reddish due to burst blood vessels under the skin. The reference wasn't to mucus either, as that plague wasn't respiratory. In fact, fever, and blood cells, and vessels bursting were about the only symptoms.

No, the green in the green fever plague didn't refer to a symptom. It didn't even have anything to do with the name of the first person to get it. It was green because it was the plague after the red plague, which had been after the blue plague. The Apocalypse Amelioration Agency had started naming plagues by color to keep them straight, all based on the ordering of a color wheel.

Not that it'd helped much. There had been several green plagues since the system had gone into use. No matter how big the color wheel, there was bound to be unrelated repetition. And, once it started repeating, there was no more sense in calling one red and another blue than there was in calling them all the plague.

Marshall thought it would have been better, if you were going to color code plagues, to at least classify colors based on symptom or causation, or level of virulence, or perhaps average mortality rate.

For example, red could be for blood plagues and blue for body temperature regulation plagues. Yellow could be the respiratory system plagues, of which there were quite a few. Then people would know what kind of plague was at hand based on the color. Perhaps they could act accordingly, such as covering their mouths more during yellow plagues to hinder spread.

But, the suggestion Marshall submitted regarding color-coding had not been adopted.

Though bursting blood vessels and fever had been the only symptoms of the green fever plague, those had been more than enough to qualify as a plague. Marshall got that one, along with most of the rest of the planet, and it was sort of like bleeding from every part of your body at once without any of it going anywhere. Just purple and red bruises all over, nothing to bandage or staunch. Quick death from lack of oxygenation and several other things.

But, it wasn't really a plague. It hadn't been caused by a bacterium or virus. It didn't even spread from person to person.

Marshall thought that was part of the definition of a plague.

Instead, it had been a mass vitamin deficiency. A new synthetic grain had been introduced into the food supply lacking a basic building block for blood vessel and cell walls. Absent that block, walls weakened and randomly burst. Due to the rapid adoption of the grain glucol, designed to serve all of the functions of gluten without any of the allergy or intolerance, and the central part of the average diet it occupied, the deficiency appeared to spread like a plague. Really, it was simply a large number of related yet isolated incidences occurring at approximately the same time.

Still, the agency had taken care of it quick enough. Booster shots of the correct missing amino acid were the immediate fix, a supplement mandated by law as an additive to glucol took care of the rest. People ceased bleeding inside all the time without good reason.

That was the last apocalypse before the immediate one, Marshall was almost certain. The existence of humanity had been threatened. Millions must have died or been close to doing so, all that sort of thing. The agency, of course, handled things.

What was the first apocalypse though? The first time mankind faced extinction and life had changed forever? Marshall tried to remember.

There had been the nuke. That one was almost mythical as far as apocalypses went. Some apocalypses came and went, never to be mentioned again, but the nuke was the apocalypse by which all other apocalypses were measured.

Could it have been the first? Or, had it made the ones before seem less like apocalypses and more like ordinary problems? Marshall wasn't sure. He'd been only a kid.

It hadn't been a war. Sure, there had been threats of war. Sure, people stockpiled nukes as if they were going to use them, but a cult had been responsible for the nuke. In fact, it was one guy with a bomb who promised everyone they were going to be purified by the eternal glow of the Lord. It was all him, building the bomb and setting it off in a major populated area.

Contrary to what might be expected, the guy hadn't gotten the nuke from a military installation. That guy refined it himself. Thorium from gas lamp mantles, advanced to weapons-grade uranium using a homemade beta cannon constructed from a block of lead, and old radium watch hands. The reports detailed the operation pretty specifically, perhaps because people marveled at how elaborate the plan had been.

Somehow, the guy pulled it off. One man, one bomb.

Marshall didn't remember what the city was called where it had gone off. Wherever it had been, that was the last of it. Nothing was left.

Granted, the bomb hadn't been very big, or particularly powerful. It wasn't a missile level nuke. The bomb itself only took out a couple hundred thousand people though it picked up more from radiation poisoning.

No, the real event was something unforeseen.

The bomb ended up being the catalyst.

Due to rising global temperatures, an atmospheric sun shield was developed and deployed. It was impressive. They created a stable, artificial gas layer as a blanket around the planet to mute solar radiation to a tolerable level. It was an artificial ozone in effect, though considerably more complex in implementation. Marshall barely grasped the compounds and isotope interactions. It was intricate, but it worked.

Of course, no one had thought to test the system under conditions of a nuclear blast. No one expected a nuclear bomb to go off, so there was no reason to consider the effects. The system was supposed to be inert, and there was simply no indicator a nuclear event would constitute special operating conditions.

Perhaps the fact even the shield system designers weren't entirely certain how the system functioned should have tipped someone off. After all, if they didn't know entirely how it worked, how could they predict what it would do in various situations? Like when some nut blows up a bomb?

But, evidently the decision had been made that combatting the rising temperatures was worth the risk of an unexplained system. The known evil was presumed worse than the unknown, potential evil one. They knew it worked. Maybe, at the time, that was enough.

Later, people would know better. They'd know the solar radiation diffusion component of the system would, in addition to dissipating the energy of the sun by spreading the affected area around the globe, contaminate the whole planet with the poison from the nuclear blast, like a contaminated Santa Claus, going down all the chimneys in the world at the exact same time. No naughty or nice list though. Death was packaged equally for all.

The blast altered the composition of the gas layer in an ironic way. Instead of acting as a filter, it operated as a magnifier. Temperatures rose tenfold faster than they had prior to the shield system. Lakes dried. Flesh baked. Unprotected skin blistered after minutes of sun exposure instead of hours.

The fix took a while. Luckily, the changed system wasn't as stable as it was originally. Eventually, the altered gas dissipated. Temperatures fell. Whether from the planetary climate cycle or from decreased industrial activity, things became cooler than they had been before it all started. People rebuilt.

Still, as long as it took to recover from the blast, Marshall wasn't sure he would have classified it as the worst. There were so many apocalypses. He wasn't sure how something like that should be defined. Technically, all the apocalypses risked the fate of humanity. Each was something capable of killing everyone and was functionally equivalent to something capable of killing everyone ten times over. After events proceeded to a certain point, differences were meaningless.

Was something capable of killing only the humans less of an apocalypse than something capable of wiping out all life on earth? If it didn't kill everybody, which it never had, did it matter how long it had taken to resolve? Was that the measure? Was it how many dead, human or otherwise? Was it how much life had changed? What were the significant factors to evaluate?

To Marshall, apocalypses seemed pretty interchangeable. Most had the possibility killing all people. After that, distinctions were nit picking.

Then there was the asteroid. Even Marshall thought the asteroid was notable. It was a rogue object from the Kuiper Belt, and had the possibility of smashing the planet. Nothing on earth would have survived. There wouldn't have been anything to survive upon. The vacuum of space tended to be unforgiving.

Shouldn't that sort of thing have been in a class by itself? People concerned themselves with people, which was understandable since that was where their interests lay, but all life? At the time, no one was sure there was any other life in the universe, so the destruction of earth could have meant the end of all life. The end of man, on the other hand, would have only been an epoch. There had been life before man and perhaps there would be life after. Man was only important to man.

And really, Marshall wondered, was life really a big deal when it came down to it? It mattered to him, and he wasn't anxious to give his life up by any means, but was life so important to him because he was a living thing? There was a great deal more in the universe that was not living. Stars, comets, planets. Cycles of creation and destruction. All would go on if life ceased. Was it tragic, on a truly universe-sized scale, if there was nothing capable of serving as an audience for the cosmic drama? Was it enough that it went on?

Some things seemed important to Marshall, but surely only because of who he was. Did any of it actually matter? If not, if his judgment was as valid as any other subjective judgment, since objectivity wasn't possible, didn't anything that could possibly kill him rank as high as anything else? Was a simple mugging as severe in magnitude as the entire universe winking out of existence?

But though Marshall wondered about these things, he recognized it was purely academic. In fact, he grasped it was a useless line of inquiry. He didn't think there were answers to find, and he probably wasn't the one to find them if there were. Besides, even if there were and he was, what would he do with those answers? He seriously doubted anyone would listen, or that such could be put to any kind of practical use.

Of course, that didn't stop his wondering. Marshall couldn't help himself. Also, there wasn't a lot for him to do which was truly useful anyway.

The asteroid, as one might have expected, did not destroy the earth. The agency had constructed their own asteroid out of space debris, and shot it at the actual asteroid, deflecting its trajectory. It had passed close enough to cause a separate tidal wave apocalypse via its gravitational pull, but that was dealt with utilizing other measures. In the end, all was well.

Actually, the asteroid had provided the impetus for dealing with yet another apocalypse, the space debris apocalypse. It was all the leftover crap people had left up there. Satellites, old rocket booster engines, space burials from when it was in vogue, garbage jettisoned from the planet when that was in vogue, and so on. There had been a ton of debris orbiting out there. Some fell in and burned up on reentry, but nowhere near enough.

It became quite a problem. Leaving the planet had become difficult. Not only did you need the correct launch window, you also had to plan to exit through a narrow gap in all the crap. At the speeds involved, even a stray fountain pen could cause irreparable horror on your space craft. You didn't want to contemplate a collision with one of the abandoned space stations.

Regardless, all that junk was swept up and neatly disposed of when the agency took care of the asteroid apocalypse. It was a clever repurposing of newly developed artificial gravity fields which rounded up the trash in orbital sweeps. Launches due to floating trash had been difficult, but were not yet impossible. Once the garbage was collected, the upper atmosphere cleared again, and the planet's leftover nuclear waste, still another apocalypse all its own, went toward a fusion reaction that welded it into a unified mass. The agency neatly arranged things so the fusion reaction provided the thrust for the artificial asteroid.

Collect, fuse, shoot. The little ball went right for the intruder asteroid and did its job. No muss, no fuss. For once, the solution didn't create any further apocalypses to deal with. It was one of the better plans the agency came up with.

Still, objects tend to orbit. There was the possibility the junk ball could return one day. Head straight for earth. Or, perhaps the asteroid would eventually correct itself from its little push and resume its earth-destroying original path. However, that day had yet to arrive. The agency tended to save tomorrow for tomorrow.

In any event, Marshall couldn't see how it still affected people. Self-preservation made as much sense as ever, but any kind of emotional reaction to an apocalypse seemed ludicrous.

An apocalypse wasn't a significant event if it was apocalypse all the time.

The earthquake apocalypse.

The asteroid apocalypse.

The green plague apocalypse.

The solar apocalypse.

The nuke apocalypse.

The warming apocalypse.

The red plague apocalypse.

The blue plague apocalypse.

The yellow plague(s) apocalypse.

The garbage apocalypse.

The nuclear waste apocalypse.

The agency strike apocalypse, combatted by the formation of an identical yet different agency, of course.

The rain of fire apocalypse.

It was constant.

How could it provoke a reaction anymore? Marshall didn't get it, he just didn't. Frankly, sometimes, he kind of wished one would happen which the agency wouldn't be able to deal with. It seemed like the only way to ever be done with the whole mess.

Chapter Three

There was one apocalypse Marshall hadn't minded quite so much. That apocalypse had actually amused him a bit.

Not that he enjoyed destruction, even in such a small amount. Marshall wasn't a monster. It was the amelioration part that mostly amused him. Perhaps it was supposed to, but Marshall doubted it. The agency came off looking a bit dumb. That was the amusing part.

There hadn't been any apocalypses for a while, and life began to return to normal. People weren't getting nervous like they usually did when it went a while between apocalypses. A lull usually meant a particularly nasty apocalypse was coming. At least, that's what experience led people to expect.

For some reason though, people were calm. That's when a city of gold appeared in the sky.

At first, everyone thought it was another agency broadcast. They got ready to flee their homes, or retreat into their homes, or barricade their homes. Whatever.

But, it wasn't a broadcast. People caught on pretty quick. For one thing, it didn't fill the entire sky the way the agency broadcasts normally did. It was big, but it was just up there and stayed in one place. Broadcasts were seen everywhere, but the city was only sighted by people near it. Then word spread around the globe.

The city was strange, old, yet new. The people who could see it said it didn't look as if it had been used, but the buildings were all ancient in style. Gold bricks. Gold streets, narrow as if for walking only. That much people could see for themselves, or be told about by people with older optical home telescopes. A larger structure, sat in the center. All of the gold roads led there.

Then the voice boomed. For once, not Malcolm's.

Though the golden city could only be seen if a person was close enough, the voice was heard worldwide. Citizens on an orbital project reported they heard it. It was heard regardless of the ambient noise level. It wasn't like it was loud enough to drown other noises out. It was more like the voice was heard comfortably alongside the ambient noise, presuming the ambient noise was comfortable.

Well, perhaps comfort was only applicable to physical eardrums. A baritone voice booming out of the heavens wasn't exactly comfortable. It was soothing to hear, but the situation was unsettling.

It didn't help the voice kept going on about Abraham, and Isaac. Moses. Something about the God of your fathers and of your fathers' fathers. There were words used which people didn't understand. It was widely rumored to be the voice of God, but it didn't make a whole lot of sense. Many people thought God would have been more coherent.

The agency attempted a broadcast while the gold city was in the sky, but it didn't work well. The agency saw no reason to classify the situation as an apocalypse or to act on it, and said everyone should remain calm. Malcolm said this despite everyone already being calm. Well, Malcom sort of said it. People had to read Malcolm's lips because the broadcast audio didn't seem to work while the voice from the gold city was talking.

Only the people within viewing distance of the gold city were aware there'd been problems with the video portion of the broadcast as well. Malcolm's image didn't project onto the floating city, or even for a small distance around it. A hole had formed in that bit of the show.

Some people suggested it looked like rays of sunshine peeking through clouds. Marshall didn't think it looked like that at all, but people kept describing the sight that way.

That's when the stairs materialized.

The city was large and the staircases came down to the ground from the edges of it. Only the edges. The staircases were delicate and winding spirals. Impossibly tall or, at least, seemingly so since there they were. No one thought to fly up to the city and touch it, but the staircases seemed solid enough, and they were gold as well.

At first, no one tried going up. When asked later, and people did ask later, no one could say why they hadn't gone to investigate. They just hadn't.

The voice continued its chant all this time, almost constantly. God of your fathers and of your fathers' fathers. And all that. Covenant. Israel. Something about Elijah and Jacob. Bondage. Lengthy stories not seeming to go anywhere. An endless, or seemingly so, stream of begats and names.

Then, people started to slowly climb the stairs. At first, it was assumed people had finally gotten brave enough to investigate. However, the climbing only went up, and although the climbing was slow, it was unhesitating. Unhurried. Those who saw people climb said the climbers didn't appear to be doing it intentionally. Not that they appeared unwilling or forced. It was more like it was happening to them as opposed to something they were consciously trying to do.

People described it like sleepwalking, though the climbers had their eyes open and were smiling.

After a while, it was realized only people of Jewish heritage were on the stairs. No one had been tracking that, or even paying attention to it, so it took a while. People hadn't thought to ask, but suddenly everyone was aware this was the case.

No one was particularly worried at that point, but they were puzzled.

The climbing continued, but progress up the stairs continued to be slow. It took days for the first of the climbers to reach the city in the sky. The flow on the stairs increased, gradually, but steadily.

People of Jewish heritage began moving closer to the stairs. No one ever said they were journeying to go up the stairs. Regardless, more moved closer and took to the stairs.

It might have seemed strange people asked so few questions, but Marshall was quick to remember people usually acted as if things weren't any of their business. As such, they seemed like they were staying out of the way.

Some who climbed were religious, but others weren't. Adoptees were also on the stairs, which left it up to debate whether they had unknown Jewish heritage or not. A few people of Jewish heritage didn't go, though it was noted later the line of descent in such cases often went through the father's side of the family.

In any event, a lot of people went.

Marshall remembered it was all pretty calm. The event eventually finished. The stair traffic trickled, and then stopped. The voice in the sky went quiet all of a sudden though the sound of distant singing could be heard from time to time. Then, after a period of time, which no one could later agree upon, the staircases were gone. As mysteriously as they had come. The golden city disappeared one day as well. If it hadn't been for all the missing people, it might have seemed like it hadn't happened.

The whole thing was pretty odd for an apocalypse, but as soon as the golden city was gone, people started feeling like it had been one. After all, a significant portion of the human population, of the shared human history, was gone. They left. Influenced by whatever it was, or not, no one knew. Regardless, people were gone. That part was easily agreed upon.

Still, no one had died. There was no widespread destruction.

That's when the locusts came.

Oddly, there hadn't been locusts living on earth then, as far as the scientists knew. It was believed the species had gone extinct a while before, perhaps in one or more of the previous apocalypses. They all died off.

Then the locusts came in clouds, millions of them, enough to darken the sun. Locusts came out of nowhere, almost as if they'd been laying eggs for generations and none of them could hatch until that exact moment. Then they all did hatch, simultaneously, as fully formed adult locusts.

Then there were famines, strangely, since the locusts couldn't have had anything to do with that. All food production was done in orbital hydroponic gardens. The low gravity vegetation mutation apocalypse hadn't happened yet, and the locusts were all on the planet surface, so they couldn't get to the fields, but the fields looked as if they'd been eaten.

It was inexplicable famine.

Weather patterns went nuts too. The moon parked itself in front of the sun and was apparently unwilling to move, plunging much of the planet into endless cold night. At the same time, thermal vents on the ocean floor shot out superheated currents, boiling the sea. Milk curdled in the refrigeration units. Burning fires froze.

There were even reports of raining frogs in some parts of the world, but that might not have been related. There was enough to worry about without bothering to check on something far away. For one thing, the frogs were edible. No one looked twice at free food all around them.

Soon though, the Apocalypse Amelioration Agency had taken care of most of the weather and food hiccups. Predators were introduced to bring the locusts under control. Gravitational manipulation devices got the moon moving again. Immense chiller units sealed the thermal vents. Everything fell into place after that.

Crops were replanted and the famines ended. Life went on. If the world was supposed to end after the construction of New Jerusalem, perhaps the golden city wasn't actually New Jerusalem. That was the only conclusion people could come to since obviously life on earth still existed.

However, the agency didn't stop there. They addressed all of the crises people were concerned with, but some must have felt it wasn't enough. The Jews were still gone, and though that part had been peaceful enough, Marshall did admit the exodus had been an apocalypse.

What could the agency do? The only way to return things to the way life had been before would have been to get the Jews back, but no one knew where they went. It wasn't a simple matter of building long-distance cruisers to explore space, locating the new home they'd gone to, and persuading them to rejoin the rest of humanity. They might have been in another universe, or another dimension. They might not even have existed at all anymore, not as anyone understood being. There was no way of knowing, and no way in which to proceed.

That's when things got entertaining.

Well, Marshall found it entertaining. He wasn't sure if anyone else was amused. Perhaps the agency wasn't, or whoever had specifically been in charge of that particular portion of the project. It hadn't made the agency look particularly capable.

Then again, Marshall didn't know what the goal had really been. Perhaps the agency, or whoever in it, had been screwing around. Maybe they had a situation that couldn't be fixed and they decided to have some fun with it. Everyone plays the clown from time to time.

But, that's when the agency decided to fake the Jews.

The agency employed a number of citizens to be Jews. It was a job, same as farming, or construction. These people were supposed to fill the gap in society formerly occupied by those who had gone, play their role.

Unfortunately, it turned out people didn't know anywhere near as much about the Jews as they'd thought they did, whether as a religion, or a group of people, or whatever. It struck Marshall as bizarre. How could an entire group of people, one as large and quite as diverse, who had been around for so long, be so poorly understood? Even with all the works describing them?

No one could, not really, describe what the Jews were. Not any of them. Individual people could be remembered and described, but the idea of Jew was elusive. What the agency had was a grasp of the impression of Jew, and that wasn't remotely the same thing.

It wasn't even close.

It was like a painting of a photocopy of a written description, a caricature, a collection of memories and characteristics, sketch lines. A group of blind men feeling up an elephant. Memory had not yet faded so badly that anyone could ignore the fact it was all completely wrong.

They taught some people to speak Yiddish, or Hebrew, and some who only sprinkled either into conversations in other languages. Still, it was only people speaking languages. It didn't seem to mean the same thing anymore. It was a performance, and it ended up coming off that way.

Restaurants, certain ones, though not many, were paid to serve kosher meals. No pork. No meat with cheese. No shellfish. All meat derived from animals slaughtered in a particular manner. No one could remember much more, though they were sure there was more to it. All that remained was a partial set of rules, monitored by no one, followed hollowly.

People ate a meal from a kosher menu, but that wasn't the same thing as someone eating kosher. The idea of kosher held on out of a desire for preservation, but it wasn't connected to anything.

Matzo, in particular, did not fare well. Everyone remembered matzo, being one of the first things they thought of when they thought of kosher food. The flour turned out funny though. The agency knew wheat, and they knew unleavened, but apparently important specifics were missing. The whole concoction turned out strange, different, though no one could put their finger on what the difference was. Flatter maybe, denser. Less taste.

The agency actually made people wander around in Hasidic regalia. Dark coats with somber hats and dangling curls, with copies of the Torah, and portions of the Talmud. The actors didn't actually read the texts, but they did pretend to. In fact, most went about their normal day. It was all just done in dress, like a costume party.

The exercise was a total failure.

Instead of making it seem like those with Jewish heritage weren't gone, the attempt emphasized the absence. People couldn't ignore what had happened when they saw the various actors wandering around and pretending to be Jews. Marshall thought it would have been better not to do anything.

Eventually, the agency gave up. The faux Jews slowly disappeared, returning to whatever occupations they'd performed before. In general, people avoided bringing up the episode. No official statement was ever issued. One day, the last pretend Jew was gone.

The Jews, the real ones, never returned.

Chapter Four

It was peaceful when Marshall awoke. Dark and peaceful. Gradually, as he came further into consciousness, he thought about how he was in his bed, in his apartment, comfortable. No apocalypse for weeks. He'd do what he was ordinarily supposed to do. Go to work if it was a workday.

The day would be an ordinary day. He hadn't woken up fully enough yet to remember what day it was. Regardless, he'd have a normal routine to go about.

That's when he noticed he couldn't see his time screen.

In fact, it was completely dark in his apartment, which wasn't right. It was never completely dark. He turned out the lights and put the shields over the windows when he slept, but his time screen always glowed. The charging indicator on his personal hygiene unit, an all-in-one bladeless razor, touchless tooth sanitizer, and various other functions Marshall never used, should have been flashing a dim green light. So should have a number of other devices that had tiny lights that never turned off. His communication module and his food preparation station were all dark, too.

Marshall groaned.

It was another power apocalypse.

He sat up in bed, and thought about it. The power was out, that was clear enough by the dark time screen. It could have meant a simple power outage instead of an apocalypse level event, but apocalypses happened more often than blackouts. Regardless, Marshall could already tell from where he was this was more annoying than the last apocalypse where the power grid went dark.

For one thing, some of his devices were battery powered. Charge lights may not have been going if a power substation went down, but status lights were connected to internal batteries and should have still been active. Batteries would run out eventually, but he doubted he'd been asleep that long.

No, something had drained all the power. Drained it, or otherwise rendered it non-functional. The exact specifics were unimportant.

Electromagnetic pulse? That was possible. He'd heard those could knock out even independently powered electronics though he wasn't entirely sure how that worked. Some sort of power sucker, stealing the juice away to somewhere else? A breakdown in the operation of electricity itself?

The possibilities were limitless or, they were while he was still on his bed not investigating. He'd have to go out and look at the sky and wait for Malcolm's announcement to elaborate the problem.

If the Apocalypse Amelioration Agency was able to send out a message. Surely the equipment for that required power. Doubtless they'd find a way around needing power for the equipment, but that could take time. Information might not be immediately forthcoming, Marshall realized.

At the same time, he decided he didn't want to know. It didn't matter. Safety procedures were the same regardless of the cause. The actual details were only drama to get caught up in.

Also, Marshall realized he could pretend it was merely an outage if he didn't know specifics. No apocalypse at all. Even in a blackout, people could still accomplish their daily tasks. Lack of power for a couple hours wasn't an excuse to be idle. A power apocalypse would be, but Marshall didn't have to think about that.

He got out of bed.

Getting ready to go out puzzled him. Personal hygiene was problematic since the unit wasn't functional. Also, the bathing apparatus wouldn't work, and he wouldn't be able to see to use it anyway. He wouldn't be able to find clothes either though that was easily handled by the fact he was still dressed from the day before.

No matter. It wouldn't be breaking routine too much to go out unwashed in mildly soiled clothing. He'd done that when he woke up late for work hung over before. He doubted anyone else would be looking their best either. The slept-in look would likely be popular.

Luckily, Marshall's front door had a manual release. All dwellings did after one of the other power apocalypses trapped people indoors for several days. He crept over his stuff carefully in the dark and popped the door open.

Luckily again, Marshall's apartment was only a single large room. It was temporary housing, one in a long line of temporary domiciles, since his actual home had been destroyed in a ball lightning apocalypse. Supposedly, he'd have a real house again someday if there was ever enough time between apocalypses to build one. Still, since it was only him, and since cooking and bathing were performed using apparatuses instead of dedicated rooms, and since he didn't accumulate much because it was so often destroyed, he didn't need more than one big room. One room was easier to get out of when an apocalypse inevitably knocked out the lights. No maze to wander around in.

Popping the door open didn't change much. It was still dark. The hallway had no windows. Marshall didn't know if it was day or night. Still, the hallway was empty so it was easy to crawl along on the carpet, easy to find the exit to the familiar emergency exit stairs, and easy to follow the guide rail down to get outside.

Easy. This was a normal day with minor inconveniences.

Marshall wondered why he didn't encounter anyone else in the hallway. Nobody crying, and wailing. It was nice. He enjoyed it. Maybe everyone was still asleep. Or, maybe he'd overslept and was the latecomer to the emergency. It might even have been that everyone else decided to sit at home in the dark. Marshall wasn't sure, but if the hallway was calmer than usual then he wasn't going to complain about it.

The quiet ended when Marshall got outside.

It took him a moment to be able to see, coming out of darkness into blazing sunlight, but there was no way to miss the commotion. There was the wailing, the metaphorical gnashing of teeth and rending of garments. Until he could see, it was only noise which came from everywhere at once. Windows were smashed, and were buildings on fire. People desperately tried to use dead devices. It was the end of the world, again.

It was pretty much what he expected.

Despite the problems everywhere, it wasn't bad. There were the regular riots and violence, but the streets were passable. The transport pods didn't work without power, but he could walk. No reason not to go about his day.

He was disappointed though when he remembered it was his day off. He couldn't ignore the apocalypse and go into work if he had no job to go to. Not that it would have worked out for him to go in. Without power, the assembly line would be motionless and there would be nothing for Marshall to do. Staying at home due to apocalypse wouldn't have been much different.

However, Marshall could make his grocery run. Being on foot would limit what he could carry, but he had nowhere to store perishables anyway. That would lighten his load a bit.

He hoped the food distributor was open, and it hadn't been burned down, and the employees bothered to show up for work. As he walked, Marshall knew the possibility of success was low. Still, that was no reason to blow off the trip, considering his other option was to stay home and freak out like everybody else. Besides, the trip itself, even if eventually fruitless, was part of his routine. He always went to the market on his day off.

The walk was pleasant when one ignored the chaos. Marshall enjoyed it. He ignored the screams from people who didn't need help anyway. He looked at things that weren't broken or aflame to avoid seeing those that were. It almost made the world better, without actually being arrogant enough decide what was better and for whom.

Eventually, he reached the food distributor. No issues. No attacks by roving bands of miscreants, no objects blocking the way, no strange items falling from the sky. It was a refreshing walk, bordered by miscellaneous insanity.

However, Marshall was unable to tell if the store was open or not.

The lights were not on, and the main sign wasn't illuminated, but the power was gone so that wasn't dispositive. He didn't see anyone inside, and no one came or went, but the security gates weren't in place. The powered glass door was open a crack.

Marshall shrugged. He'd only find out if he went inside. He might as well try.

It wasn't quite as simple as he hoped. The huge door was open a crack, but not wide enough to admit his slightly oversized frame. It was suitable for someone more slender, someone smaller.

He figured he'd try to push the door open. There were scuff marks on the ground, suggesting someone else tried to open the door too. The door was heavy, but Marshall either had to push or go home, and he wasn't ready to go home yet.

He worked his shoulder into the gap of the doorway and heaved. His face reddened and he puffed as beads of sweat dotted his forehead. Though normally motor controlled, the giant door was on rollers for sliding and began to move. Marshall focused on his task so much he didn't notice when he'd moved the door enough for him to pass through.

Standing to catch his breath a moment, he looked at what he'd done. It wasn't much of an accomplishment, but he'd done something. Accomplishments were few and far between in an age of apocalypses.

As he went inside, he was less convinced than ever the food distributor was open. It was deserted. But worrying about open or closed was merely semantics. He figured he'd grab his groceries first and then see if there was a way to pay.

That's when the display stack of creamed corn canisters next to him exploded. Marshall dove for the floor. His ears rang from the blast and he could smell something sulfurous. That, and corn. Canisters and fragments of canisters clattered to the floor around him. He was wet with the creamed mush. He hoped that was all it was. He didn't think he'd been hit. Nothing hurt, but maybe he was in shock.

Looking up, he saw a slight woman standing a little way away pointing an odd-looking weapon at him. The thing was black and long like a shock rifle, but didn't look remotely electric. The gun was made of pipes, one main one, and some kind of grip. Little cartridges ran all up and down the sides. Smoke trailed out of the end, which the woman was still pointing at him.

"Looting is not allowed in the distributorship," the woman shouted. She had long hair so blond it was almost white.

Marshall wasn't sure if she was an employee. Normally, employees wore special jumpers. Then again, normally, they didn't usually fire weapons at him.

The woman pulled a secondary grip near the pointing end of the weapon. It slid back and then forward again with a chhk-cchhhhk sound and a little canister shot out the side. "Though distributorship policy does not condone looting of any kind, if you must loot we ask you do it at another location. Thank you for your patronage and please have a pleasant day."

"What the hell are you doing?" Marshall wiped creamed corn from his face. "I'm not looting, I'm shopping."

The woman looked puzzled. "Our credit processing systems are not operational. Do you have non-electronic funds for payment?"

"Yes."

The woman angled the weapon away from him though she still held it at the ready. "All right, then. Proceed. However, please refrain from opening the refrigeration cabinets. We still hope the items inside won't spoil before power is restored."

Marshall nodded and got up from the floor. He wiped corn off of himself as he stood. It didn't make him any more presentable, but the soiled state of his clothing was certainly no longer noticeable.

"I'm Marshall, by the way," he told her, offering her his hand. She didn't take it.

"Bonnie."

"Why are you yelling?"

"New distributorship policy. Today there is only yelling in the distributorship. No inside voices permitted."

"Okay. Did you just make that up?"

She shrugged. "Yeah. Why not? I'm the only one who came to work. I keep the place safe from looting. I get to make the rules. That's how it works."

Marshall looked at the exploded creamed corn canisters. "Maybe they'd have been better off if they'd been looted."

"Can't make an omelet without taking a shotgun to some creamed corn," she responded. "Are you going to shop or not? I'd tell you I don't have all day, but I kind of do. I guess, I'm only curious."

Shotgun? Is that was that thing was? Marshall guessed so. Whatever it was, it must have been an antique.

He grabbed an item carrier and began wandering the aisles. Since perishables were out, both by practicality and proscription, he'd need to get some dry goods he didn't normally purchase. Dehydrated potato wafers. Preserved beef strips. It felt a bit like camping, or he presumed it did. No one camped anymore.

The woman followed him around the store with the shotgun. She didn't point it at him, but she stalked around as if she might at any moment. She tried not to appear interested in Marshall's shopping, but she kept a close eye on him.

"So why'd you pick an apocalypse as a time to go shopping?" Bonnie cocked her head sideways.

"I'd never get any shopping done if I waited till there wasn't an apocalypse, would I?"

Her eyes widened in surprise. Hazel.

"Besides, I didn't have to go to work today. That means time for shopping. I even thought about going to work, if there'd been anything to do on the line. I'm temporarily in a factory until they get the design division up and running again. Frankly, I'm bored. Apocalypses are boring."

Bonnie nodded. Her eyes never left Marshall, though she stopped brandishing the gun and slung it over her shoulder.

"Obviously," she yelled. "I know what you mean."

It took Marshall a couple circuits around the distributorship to find everything he thought he'd need. It wasn't much, only one item carrier full, but he didn't know where everything was kept since it wasn't his usual batch of purchases. Seeking and searching took time, and he wasn't in much of a hurry while walking with Bonnie.

She seemed pretty patient about it as well. She strolled around the distributorship with him, walking when he walked, and stopping when he stopped. When he finished, she led him up to the front and tallied the total by hand.

"Seventy-five credits." she yelled, holding out her hand.

He paid her. Luckily, he had bills for the exact amount. He was sure there was change in the transaction terminals, but those were all dead. Marshall had no idea if the money storage compartments could be accessed manually. He could have told her to keep the change, but he had no idea how long his paper credits would have to last. It was nicer not to tax his supply any more than necessary.

"I can't enter your transaction into the rewards program to get you your points right now, because the system is obviously down," she yelled. "Write down your name and home location on this slip and I'll get it all entered once we're back online."

Marshall took the paper she handed him and did as he was told, though he wasn't worried about reward points. Still, it was another little bit of normalcy. Whether or not she was doing it to make him feel better, it was a nice touch.

Bonnie helped him package up his haul. Then she walked him back to the door, pulling it closed most of the way after him. He decided she must have been considerably stronger than she looked.

"Thank you for shopping with us today," she yelled through the door gap. "It may be the apocalypse out there, but it's everyday low prices in here."

Chapter Five

A siren sounded from Marshall's communication unit. That alone wasn't a surprise because the power had been back on for weeks. Marshall hadn't paid attention to the provided explanation. It was something about physical properties reversing or electrons flowing the other way. Whatever it was hadn't made much sense, and smacked heavily of pseudoscience. Marshall hadn't given a damn anyway. The apocalypse was over. There was no need to study it or mark the occasion.

Nor was it surprising the siren was for the Apocalypse Readiness System. Of course it was another apocalypse. More of those came through on Marshall's communication unit than personal communication requests. He wondered why he paid the bill for the thing.

He picked up the unit and read the text scrolling across the notification surface. No doubt Malcolm was also outside in the sky, delivering a verbatim pronouncement.

The message sounded as if it had been lifted from an old thriller program Marshall had seen back when they were running often enough to be watched regularly. He decided to read it as if it were. He wanted it to be entertaining instead of depressing.

Citizens, the earth is being terrorized by a virtual army of undead assassins. The dead have risen from their graves and are wreaking havoc upon the living. The cause is unknown at this time, but an investigation is ongoing.

Citizens are advised to stay in their homes. All nonessential businesses and government services are suspended until further notice. Updates will follow and those classified as essential personnel will be notified separately.

Do not panic. All will be well.

Warning, some of the dead are visibly identifiable, and are easily avoided. However, others may be freshly dead and are significantly more difficult to identify. For safety, do not approach any person acting strangely, or unusually sluggish, particularly those unable to speak.

At this time, there is no evidence this condition is contagious by bite or other delivery mechanism. As such, the danger is likely small as long as the dead are avoided.

Please do not form zombie-killing parties. The Apocalypse Amelioration Agency is on top of the situation, and vigilante activity increases the likelihood of mistaken identification and unintended death.

Thank you for your cooperation.

Marshall set aside the communication unit.
Zombies.

Oh yeah, people were going to remain calm. They always took sane and rational approaches to apocalypses. Surely they'd be even more orderly when faced with the living dead. He grimaced, unable to find amusement in his own sarcasm.

No work, again. The factory would be shut up tight. No way of acting as if it were business as usual.

He went back to bed.

⚓ ⚓ ⚓

Marshall was awakened by a knock at the door. He sat upright, puzzled.

Wasn't everyone supposed to stay inside? Who could possibly be looking for him? Had someone suddenly decided he was essential and needed to go to work, and made a personal appearance to deliver the news? Zombies didn't knock, did they?

Marshall figured there was only one way to find out. He opened the door.

The girl from the distributorship stood in the doorway. Bonnie. Her long blond hair was tied up in a bun and she had on stretchy tight black tank top and pants. She was also holding a pair of kinetic rifles.

"Hey," he said, at a loss for anything else to say.

"Come on," she nodded her head toward the hallway. She shifted the straps of a large carry pack fixed to her back. "Let's get going."

"What?" Marshall blinked. "Where are we going? How did you know where I lived?"

Bonnie rolled her eyes. "You didn't really think I was going to enter all that in to get you shopping points, did you, Lunk? I thought we'd go on a date, and what better time than now for a picnic?"

"Picnic?" Marshall was floored.

"Sure." She shifted the carry pack again by way of demonstration. "Got all the stuff right here. It's a great day out there, even if it's a little heavy on the zombie side. I guarantee the parks won't be crowded though. Not with live people, anyway."

"What about the zombies?" Marshall was still having trouble with the idea of a zombie picnic. "How'd you get through?"

Bonnie smirked. "You can run, can't you? They can't. Just don't go anywhere you can get pinned down. It's not hard and there's not that many of them. Don't be stupid, Lunk, and you'll be fine."

Marshall just stood there and looked at her.

"Aaaagh! I'm not suicidal," she said. "I just don't want to stay in and think about zombies all day. I want us to go on a simple, run of the mill picnic."

"I don't have a death wish either," Marshall explained, "I just—"

She tossed him one of the kinetic rifles. "Come on, then. If one gets too close, that'll drive it back again. Break open a hole to run through if you get surrounded. Don't be a pussy, Lunk."

Lunk? What was that about? Short for lunkhead? He wasn't dumb, was he? He had advanced engineering degrees from back when they still had universities. He'd told her his name, right? What was up with the endearingly insulting nickname?

But, what else could he do? He followed her.

A zombie apocalypse day picnic.

To give Bonnie credit, there weren't too many zombies out on the street. Rotting housewives, office drones, construction workers, all that. Most were pretty obvious, fairly decomposed. Not all were, but Marshall and Bonnie didn't see many of the living outside. The zombie shamble was unmistakable.

The zombies noticed them pretty quickly so Bonnie made no real attempt to stay quiet. The zombies noticed, and lurched toward Bonnie and Marshall, but never had an opportunity to get close. Bonnie changed course to avoid the ones in front, and those behind fell further back. There were clusters, but groups were as slow as individuals so that wasn't a problem either. Bonnie kept to open areas so there was plenty of room to maneuver.

"No transport pods?" Marshall asked after they'd walked for a while. "Are we going somewhere close?"

Bonnie shook her head. "Not really, but walking is better. You want to be trapped in a box right now? I don't. Anyway, the transport pods are probably out of service."

Marshall hadn't thought about that though he should have. He wasn't paying enough attention.

A zombie popped up from a pile of trash in front of Bonnie, too close for her to run. The thing seemed to have been lying under there waiting, but Marshall didn't think zombies could plan. Maybe it just arose, having been dead in the trash from a previous apocalypse.

Bonnie didn't pause to debate the issue. She engaged the contact plates on the kinetic rifle.

The air between the rifle and the zombie shimmered. It looked like boiling water, but in the air. Then the zombie flew back, crumpling like he'd been kicked in the chest. His arms and legs snapped forward and there was a sound akin to tearing sheet metal.

The zombie shot back about thirty or forty feet, stopping only when he slammed into a skiffer service station wall. The impact was accompanied by the crunch of bone and the squish of whacked flesh. As the zombie slid to the ground, a trail of blood smeared down the wall. Blood spilled out of various portions of the zombie as well. The weapon may have been clean, but the results weren't.

"Neat," Marshall quipped.

"Told you these worked fine," Bonnie retorted. She only then lowered the kinetic rifle.

The zombie stayed balled up in a heap, but it then struggled to get to its feet. The zombie's bones were clearly broken, as the zombie's legs didn't much support it anymore and its arms hung askew. One arm drooped lower than the other and its shoulders were crooked as if its rib cage was no longer symmetrical. Though slower than before, it again began making its way toward Marshall and Bonnie.

That's when they left.

The zombie quickly fell behind. Once it was out of sight, Marshall and Bonnie slowed to a normal pace.

Bonnie led Marshall to a park. It was a pretty nice one, a green space set aside so families could pretend to get back to nature. Also, it helped with the water drainage problems the extensive pavement caused. The park had some open areas, strips of trees here and there, and some sections with playground equipment. There was a spot specially set up for picnics though Bonnie wisely didn't head there. For one thing, the picnic grounds were full of zombies.

In fact, there were zombies all over the park. There weren't as many as there had been through the city blocks they walked, but there weren't many obstructions in the park. They could see a lot farther and thus could see a lot more zombies at one time. A lot more.

Of course, seeing a lot more zombies involved a lot more zombies seeing them. The situation went both ways. More zombies able to see them led to more zombies heading for them. A herd, tracking in from all directions. Even the kinetic rifles could only to do so much.

Marshall was starting to see a big problem with the picnic idea. Zombies were easy enough to avoid as long as they stayed on the move. The gathering would get too thick if Bonnie and Marshall sat down, such as for a picnic lunch.

Did Bonnie intend to eat while walking around, a picnic on the move? Marshall thought he could see how that might work, but it didn't sound like much fun. Or, much like a normal day.

But, Bonnie didn't take out any food as they strolled. She headed right for the pond in the park. There was a little greenish water and a pleasant man-made island in the center, complete with a few trees and bushes. It wasn't a big island, but it was nicely landscaped to be visually appealing.

"Put these on," Bonnie said, removing a couple pairs of foot-sized electronic devices from her carry pack. "Then follow me."

Marshall realized they were hydrophobic field generators. Old ones. Marshall had only seen the like in museums. Near shore fisherman supposedly used to use them to walk around on the top of water while fishing, back when there were still fish in the tidal areas. The various oil spill apocalypses had taken care of that. There wasn't a whole lot of use for the things anymore, so they weren't commonly around.

Accordingly to what Marshall had heard though, the disc shaped fields put out by the devices repelled water so strongly the wearer would never break the water's surface tension. The dimension of the field provided balance. The toy appealed to Marshall, even if it wasn't particularly useful anymore.

Bonnie activated the devices and made sure Marshall's were on correctly. He couldn't see any difference, but he could feel a light vibration and hear a quiet throbbing noise.

Bonnie walked out onto the water. "Come on," she shouted.

Tentatively, he stepped out after her. The experience was unsettling. The water wasn't turbulent by any means, being a tiny little pond, but it certainly wasn't still. Regardless, it smoothed to a glass sheet a certain distance around each foot wherever he stepped. It was weirder when his feet came close together, the smoothed area forming the outline of an infinity symbol.

Still, he didn't fall in. He stayed upright and walked up to Bonnie on the island.

"Take 'em off now," she ordered. "The charge cells don't last long anymore and we'll eventually want to walk back across. You could swim, I suppose, but I wouldn't. The water's full of duoose crap."

He did as instructed. Bonnie began taking food out of her carry pack. It was quite an assortment. Fried chicourkey legs, some kind of casserole with vinegared carrots and fresh green peas, and dehydrated potato wafers. She even had flavored sweet water pods. Bonnie apparently believed in being prepared. There was a lot more, a lot after Marshall stopped trying to note it all. A lot of a lot of stuff.

"Planning to feed the zombies?" Marshall joked. "I'm not quite that hungry."

"It may not only be for today," she countered, pointing out at the shore. "I figured we might be stuck here until the apocalypse was over once we got across."

Marshall's eyes followed her finger. Sure enough, the shore teemed with zombies. Uncountable numbers of zombies, milling about as they were, and more kept coming. They were thick enough Bonnie and Marshall couldn't see the park for a good ways off from the pond.

Bonnie and Marshall settled in and started to eat.

The zombies seemed shy of the water. Every once in a while, one tried to make for them and go across. But though the pond was small, it was decently deep, at least over an average person's head. The zombie would submerge as it shot forward. Then, once it lost sight of them, it would apparently forget what it was doing and eventually wander back to shore.

Marshall realized if enough tried at the same time, the pond would fill. Then the others would be able to make it across on the heads of their fellows without losing eye contact and thereby interest. However, that possibility never happened. Their shyness of the water appeared to keep the number trying to a minimum. Instead they thronged on the shore and moaned a lot.

Safe, Marshall relaxed and ate. Bonnie appeared to pay little mind to the zombies.

After they ate, they sat back in the grass and napped. Bonnie shifted over at one point and placed her head on Marshall's stomach. He liked that. He watched her head rise and fall with his breath. The day felt pleasant.

"Can you call it an apocalypse if the world doesn't really end up ending?" Bonnie spoke up.

Marshall sighed. "It does make it seem like something other than an apocalypse, doesn't it? The word should be saved for something that happens less often. This is more of an inconvenience, something like that. We should call it something that sounds less impressive."

"Yeah."

"I don't know though," he continued. "It is always the end of something. Life changes forever. Only it seems to do it pretty often."

"Everything changes every moment of every day," she countered. "That doesn't make any moment more significant than another. It's all the same."

Marshall grunted, agreeing.

"I feel like I'm always at a funeral," she went on. "Endless commemoration with no moving on. Meaningless."

Marshall frowned. There weren't funerals anymore either, he realized. He supposed people died too often, no time for formal ceremonies though he couldn't think of anyone he'd known who had died off the top of his head. Maybe it was too easy to forget, given how things were.

And the sky was full of Malcolm, Malcolm with his maroon vestments and shirt of real woven silver. Bonnie yawned. Marshall glanced at the zombies. None of the zombies looked up. The sky was none of their concern.

"Citizens." Marshall and Bonnie yelled at the same time as Malcolm, anticipating.

"Citizens. Your Apocalypse Amelioration Agency has discovered the source of this problem. All will be well quite soon, measures are being taken at this very moment. Your safety is our foremost concern."

Malcolm paused, his image gazing down at them. Marshall wondered if he was pausing for effect, letting people's reactions take hold. Marshall didn't feel anything take hold. He doubted Bonnie did either.

"A Voodoun group has rediscovered an ancient practice for raising the dead," Malcolm continued after a moment. "They hoped to take over the world. However," he smiled, "salt destroys the process. Our weather control satellites will shower the earth with a salt-water rain. Your tribulations are about to end."

Malcolm vanished. Clouds formed quickly and droplets began to fall. Marshall licked his lips: salty. He wondered what the salt would do to plant life, but doubtless that would be a worry for another day. He glanced at the zombies.

The salt did appear to have an impact. No longer did they focus on Marshall and Bonnie. They writhed as if on fire. Or rather, they writhed as if alive and on fire since fire hadn't seemed to be much of a concern before.

Zombies clawed at their own flesh, ripping open their skin and poking their own eyes out. They seemed to feel pain for the first time, or something akin to it. They almost looked as if they were exploring themselves, but in a terrified way rather than with a sense of wonder.

Marshall imagined they'd all simultaneously realized they were actually dead and couldn't process that fact. It sure looked that way. He shuddered, finding a small amount of sympathy for what he imagined they were experiencing.

One by one, the zombies collapsed. Dead, or apparently so. Dead for final, not undead. They didn't move. The rain stopped.

After a time, the park was still. It was covered wall to wall with rotting corpses, but it was still. Marshall thought it a bit gross.

Regardless, the present apocalypse had ended. They could again return to their respective homes.

Chapter Six

Marshall actually got to go to work for once. It was an odd thing to be grateful for, soldering the few non-automated board components for communication units, but he was. One chip after another, one board after another, mundane. The conveyor surface brought a partially assembled board to him. He quickly soldered on the signal decompression processor. Then the further completed board moved on down the line to the next station.

There was some sort of sensor mechanism operating which determined when Marshall was finished with his task and reactivated the conveyor surface. He didn't have to do anything. It could have been a video monitor, or the line detected when his soldering iron was idle. Maybe it was timed and Marshall didn't notice his performance was that precise. He just didn't know. He hadn't had enough workdays to play around with it and find out, or ask anyone. Work happened so rarely he was glad just to be there and worked like a machine.

The board arrived. The part placed. Soldered. The board left. Board arrived. Part placed. Soldered. Board left. Board arrived. Part placed. Soldered. Board left.

Eight hours.

The line was in a cavernous warehouse room. Tons of little stations, each in a row and each connected by the conveyor surface. Various automated stations in between. Parts came in one dark hole at one side of the line and more completed parts went out a slightly less dark hole on the other side. Not much talking, no drama. Only work getting done.

Eventually, the workday finished. Marshall wondered what the chances were he'd be back the next day. He was hopeful, but experience didn't make him overly optimistic.

Marshall left the factory. He walked to the transport pod and got inside, waiting for it to take him home.

After a while, he realized he'd been daydreaming. He did that in the transport pods sometimes since it was a self-driving vehicle. Usually he snapped out of it when he arrived home and the doors opened. However, he woke up this time because some part of his brain realized he'd been traveling longer than normal.

He probably should have figured it out sooner, given it was the same ride each time. Any difference should have been noticeable even though he rarely went to work. Plus the dinging alarm should have caught his interest.

It really wasn't an alarming noise, like a fire alert or a bomb warning, but it wasn't as mild as his communication unit alert either. He definitely should have noticed.

Especially if he intended to live. Even with the agency handling things, one needed to pay attention.

Marshall looked around.

The door to his pod was locked. Not merely fastened closed like during normal transit. The door override mechanism was fully engaged. That was only for emergencies. Various lights flashed all around. In addition to the dinging alarm, a pleasant voice calmly and repetitiously recited, "Please remain stationary. This vehicle has been commandeered by the Apocalypse Amelioration Agency."

Marshall sighed. He wondered what it was now.

The transport pod soon left his familiar neighborhood. He'd been traveling for quite a while, when he figured out he was headed for the city center.

The city center was an immense paved square, empty of all buildings and vehicles and such. Marshall supposed it was once at the actual center of the city, but that had been long ago. Given how things went, expansion wasn't likely uniform. Of course, Marshall hadn't opportunity to study recent city planning maps in relation to the center. He merely assumed.

The center was primarily used for governmental gatherings. Rallies. Mass inoculations when a plague apocalypse was ongoing.

When he arrived, the center was not devoid of all structures. Transport pods were letting people off everywhere and the center was filled. There were a number of immense flying freighters scattered throughout the expanse of the square, each at least the size of a city block, and forty stories or more tall.

Marshall wondered if they were deep space freighters. They didn't look particularly aerodynamic and were armored thickly in cerapolymer-plated steel, very thickly. Marshall found himself reminded of elephants, of which he'd only seen images. Silent and slow, unstoppable beasts. They dwarfed the people milling about.

His pod opened and agency soldiers dressed in deep blue impact armor met him at the door. They instructed him an important citizen address was to begin soon and he needed to wait at a particular designated position. They formally escorted him to a spot and ordered him to remain there.

As he waited, Marshall noticed the multitude of people weren't actually milling about as much as it had originally appeared. Most were standing still in the spots obviously designated for them. The only people milling were agency soldiers who were escorting fresh arrivals. The throng solidified increasingly as more arrivals reached their spots and stopped. No one appeared to defy the order to remain in position once escorted.

A lone skiffer was flying up and down the rows, perhaps monitoring. An audio unit mounted on the craft kept blaring: "Please remain patient. We apologize for the inconvenience. The broadcast will begin once all citizens have arrived and the assembly is fully ordered. Thank you for your cooperation."

The message sounded as if it had been designed to be soothing, but the voice was robotic and the audio unit squealed with distortion. The effect was disconcerting instead, leaving people nervous. Then again, perhaps that was the goal. Disoriented people didn't become indignant and start demanding to know what was going on and move from their places. Either way, no one moved.

After a while, people stopped arriving. The skiffer ceased its systematic buzzing around the crowd. The public address message cut off. People stood in place, looking around. It was quiet. No one talked.

Marshall was amazed by the number of people in the center, all lined up in neat little rows and columns. He swore the whole city had to be there. There were more people than he could count and they stretched out as far as he could see in any direction.

He almost laughed at how orderly the people were. He wasn't used to seeing people calm and collected. Well, collected at least. They probably weren't calm, despite their stillness.

Then Marshall saw all the necks crane upward and he realized the broadcast was starting. He'd been too busy watching people. Malcolm filled the sky.

"Citizens." Malcolm predictably boomed.

Did the speech always need to start out with citizens? Did Malcolm think people might not realize he was talking to them if that wasn't specified? The projection occupied the entire sky. People got it.

"We have taken extraordinary measures in gathering you all here. For this, we apologize," Malcolm went on. "However, we had little choice. Our current situation calls for extreme measures. Our situation is grave."

"Ah, that clears that up," Marshall quipped quietly. This apocalypse, and surely it was an apocalypse, was grave. Grave separated it from the serious apocalypses, or even the life threatening ones. Grave, why that was more earth shattering than the dire ones. Heaven help them, this one was grave. Now everyone was in trouble.

"Because of the nature of what we are asking of you," Malcolm explained, "I will be detailed. As we all know, one day our sun will progress to the next stage of its development as a star. It will transform into a red giant. In doing so, it will expand. Its heat will increase tremendously. At the same time, its mass will dissipate and the nearest planets, ours included, will begin to spiral outward."

Gasps erupted from the crowd

Really? Marshall thought. Gasps? Malcolm hadn't told them anything shocking yet. This was elementary school science so far.

"However, our planet will not spiral far enough outward. Eventually, the sun will expand to swallow the earth. Of course, before then the increased heat will destroy all life on the planet. And, to complete the picture, once the planet is within the diameter of the sun, our orbit will decay and the earth will fall into the sun's core. The destruction will be complete and total."

Malcolm paused. The crowd was silent. They hung on Malcolm's every word.

Dolts.

"We know this, and we have known it. We knew it would happen, but not for over seven billion years. However, we have recently learned it will actually happen very, very soon. We estimate we have, at most, a couple of months. Perhaps less."

People continued to listen, but no one reacted. Why not now? Marshall silently demanded. The bad news had finally been delivered. Was that not a shock? Why didn't it change anything?

"Our scientists detected an alarming rate of increase in the sun's heat. It is expanding, and expanding unimaginably fast. The helium-burning phase, precursor to red giant status, once believed to be over a hundred million years in duration, is now expected to last a matter of days. Perhaps hours. According to the rate of progression observed thus far, our planet will be uninhabitable in less than a month. We do not understand why this sudden, almost instantaneous, acceleration has occurred. All we know is it is happening."

Marshall wanted to run and start shaking people. React. Show some emotion. Don't freak out like you always do, but do something. Animate. Don't just stand there like a bunch of dolls.

He didn't. He wanted to, but he stayed put. He knew he wouldn't do it, and they wouldn't listen anyway. They didn't really listen to anything.

"We must leave our home. The Apocalypse Amelioration Agency has located another habitable world in a nearby star system. Even with our fastest freighters, this journey will take months. And though our planet may be survivable for upwards of a month, we would not travel far enough to be safe if we tarry in the slightest. We might get off world, but we would burn to death in our ships. We simply could not get far enough in time."

Malcolm paused again, this time apparently to collect himself. Marshall swore he quickly straightened his hair. Then it looked like Malcolm was overcome with emotion. Marshall couldn't be sure.

"Therefore, we must ask you to immediately board the freighters. We will depart the exact second everyone is inside. There is no time to return to your homes first, no time to collect your things. Do not try to locate your families, we must board now. This has been meticulously organized. Board the ship you are told to, and go where you are instructed. Trust that your family and whatever possessions can be saved will be waiting for you in your assigned quarters. This is the only way we can survive."

Malcolm then put his hands behind his back and puffed out his chest. His face was grim, but bore a tight smile. He nodded at the swath of people on the ground once and his image vanished.

Immediately, agency soldiers marched among the rows and directed people to ships. The process was methodical and efficient. It actually proceeded quickly. Doubtless, the spots had been determined based on planned boarding order. It looked a lot like a marching band show.

Marshall was impressed. He hadn't thought his fellow citizens capable of working together like that, of interacting in such a large scale and cooperative way. It was like they were entirely different people than those he'd known.

But, he realized they weren't really capable of such a thing. They were doing it, that was true, but they were doing what they'd been told. Each could do as ordered and no more. The agency was the real force, as it always was. The people on their own would have panicked and died.

Luckily for them, the agency was in charge at the moment.

It was Marshall's turn. Soldiers pointed him to a nearby ship. For a good portion of the way down the bare metal corridors, sterile in their lack of ornamentation, instrument, or feature of any kind, he stayed in his group. Each time they arrived at a section split, the group was divided. When he was with a cluster of only a few dozen, Marshall was directed through a doorway, alone.

The set of chambers beyond was to be his new home, for at least a few months.

He looked around. It was drab, but it wasn't too bad. Most of his stuff was there, even stuff he didn't recognize. Maybe he'd been issued extra stuff for the trip. There was definitely more furniture, though much of it looked old and cobbled together. Regardless, it was a palace compared to his one room apartment.

He hadn't needed much room before, but he couldn't go outside for a while so room would be nice. This would be it.

Marshall caught sight of a pair of hydrophobic field generators lying next to a carry pack on the floor. He quickly searched the chambers and found Bonnie lying on the bed, her hands folded over her chest, blond hair placed carefully in a fan over the pillow.

"I was wondering when you'd get here," she said.

Marshall stared. "How'd you manage this? I thought they worked out everything beforehand. You got them to switch?"

She smiled. "They wanted to keep families together. I told them we got married during the picnic and hadn't had a chance to register. Turns out, there's not much left in the way of requirements for marriage anymore."

He smiled too and sat down on the other side of the bed. He laughed. They already had their own sides.

That was fast.

Marshall wondered how much of a marriage this was to be.

"So you're in love with me now?"

She swatted him. "Not quite yet. Don't get so flattered. I just couldn't stand the idea of talking to any of those other twits for months on end."

The ship began to move.

Chapter Seven

The new planet was all right. If you'd drugged Marshall and switched him from earth without letting him know, he wasn't sure he would have been able to tell the difference at first.

At first.

He would have known it was a different city, a much newer one still under construction in many parts, but probably not much more.

There was a star that resembled the sun. Two suns actually, but only one was visible at a time and planetary orbit resulted in a day of the usual length. There was a moon, though it was an agency construct designed to make weather patterns more like earth.

Whether or not the fake weather moon worked, Marshall admitted the climate was pretty similar. The current season, or what passed for a season matched what had been going when they left earth. Warm, but not hot. A chill started creeping into the air, hinting that winter, or something like it, was on the way.

The atmosphere was different though. It turned out to be a bit richer in oxygen than Earth had been. People could breathe, but it tended to make them giddy. Oxygen toxicity was a risk, though the excess wasn't a huge amount.

The Apocalypse Amelioration Agency did something about it.

Marshall figured that was probably a good idea. He didn't think people needed to be any giddier than they already were.

The solution was to have everyone carry around little oxygen burner modules. Tiny little boxes which clipped to people's waistbands. The first designs actually produced an arc flame and a little smoke occasionally, but that was only the initial models. Improvements led to ones with no apparent flame source, smoke, or detectable heat. They appeared to do nothing, but oxygen in the immediately surrounding environment was apparently combined into various compounds in some kind of flameless incineration process.

Marshall did think the new models were better than the old, but he thought something better than burning oxygen should have been found. Perhaps some sort of other chemical reaction could reduce oxygen levels without producing fumes. Even if the new models didn't produce visible smoke, he was sure there had to be fumes. There was certainly some kind of adverse effect, Carbon monoxide perhaps.

There always was.

Marshall hadn't been part of the group that did the development, though. The design division hadn't been restarted though that was still supposed to happen at some point. The burner modules were agency products.

Instead, Marshall found himself assembling the contraptions. More assembly line work, though it wasn't soldering components. Technically, it wasn't really assembly. He calibrated the finished modules. For some reason, they hadn't been able to automate that aspect of it. Something about sensors not being able to precisely determine human comfortable ambient environment.

Though Marshall thought he could have come up with something better, at least he was working regularly. That beat the alternative.

Bonnie was assigned a different job as well, different but not so different. Instead of groceries, Bonnie was assigned clothing. She seemed okay with that and went to work every day.

Marshall thought she should have been doing assembly work of some kind, but no one asked him what he thought. He and Bonnie kept up the marriage thing and were given an apartment together. As a result, he found out more about her various projects. The shotgun?

Kinetic rifles?

Hydrophobic field generators?

She'd scavenged all those parts and broken devices from junk heaps, and brought them home to rebuild them. She didn't seem keen on constructing new things, but she loved tinkering with junk. Old stuff was a particular favorite. She had an impressive collection of strange gadgets.

Marshall knew she could have been assigned to work assembly if she wanted to be, but, some previous apocalypse shifted her from assembly to retail and she never went back.

He didn't ask her why.

He got the idea she wasn't willing to tinker for anyone but herself anymore. They weren't worthy. Except for him. Maybe. He frequently got the benefit of her completed projects. No one else though. She kept it all to herself.

He also got the idea she didn't want to talk about going back to her old job.

Still, life was peaceful.

Bonnie and Marshall were having a good time. He went to work, she went to work. They came home and hung around with each other. There were no apocalypses. Life settled into a routine. They'd both missed that, a routine.

Of course, that was only until the aliens invaded.

An alien invasion apocalypse.

Well, perhaps that terminology wasn't exactly accurate. The aliens were native to the planet, so they weren't really aliens. Marshall supposed they weren't really invaders either, since it was their planet to start with. People tended to classify things as alien or invader when they actually meant they are not us and they are against us, but Marshall thought they should have been more careful in their descriptions. The terms weren't that flexible. The phrase alien invasion apocalypse was often tossed around, but it wasn't correct.

Marshall did have to admit, though, there was a way of looking at it that made it work. Maybe it was more a question of how to group the terms than using the wrong ones.

After all, didn't it come about, the apocalypse and all, because humans came to the planet? Since they weren't natives, weren't people actually the aliens? Aliens didn't only mean others from outside. Further, they colonized a planet where something already lived. Didn't that make them invaders? Even if they weren't the ones instigating the various hostilities? At least intentionally?

If Marshall looked at it that way, Marshall thought it could be defined as an alien invasion apocalypse. It was only that life was apocalyptic for the invading aliens. In other words: humanity.

The initial assessment of the planet had been it was capable of supporting life, not that it already contained a native population. Sure, there were some plants and animals, things like that, but nothing that would supposedly require conquering. Or, more applicably, nothing likely to conquer humanity.

Of course, it was difficult to detect something that lives under the ground from at least a solar system away. The fact the worms had apparently been in some kind of hibernation for several hundred years or more didn't help matters. Also, the curious fact their flesh was somehow composed of the same material as the planet itself hid a few things from the scans. Regardless of the exact reason, no one had a clue.

The worms were there though. Giant worms. Only heaven knew how many of the things were below the surface. They were humongous though and each was at least the size of an average apartment building. They had incredibly tough bodies and an immense, toothy mouth.

It was suspected the worms felt surface vibrations and came up to blindly swallow something for dinner. A hole suddenly opening beneath a person's feet and even if the worm missed, the hole got you. When not fatal, the worm encounter still tended to scare the piss out of people.

The worm's speed was amazing, though definite figures were hard to come by. On planet there was no known scanning tech which was reliably capable of differentiating the leviathans from the rock around them. Nor was it able to effectively detect movement underground. The rock was simply too dense for fields to penetrate.

There was at least some secondary evidence of speed. It was evident in the destruction. The worms came up anywhere with almost no notice. Seismic detectors only registered activity seconds before a surfacing. The ground where tunnels had already been found, the ground where the agency said there were no tunnels, it made little difference. The worms moved pretty speedy when they were above ground.

No one was sure if human arrival is what woke them, or if the move was incredibly poorly timed. The end of hibernation could have been a coincidence. Either way, the situation wasn't good.

Worms tried to swallow people everywhere. Also, the tunnels made ground unstable. Collapses were commonplace. Almost as fast as the agency built something the structures were in ruins again. Marshall figured the loss of life and property must have been tremendous, but no exact figures were announced.

Of course, they had to go back to earth.

Well, Marshall didn't think they had to go back, but it's what they did.

The agency could have fought the worms. The agency could have exterminated them, or trimmed their population. It wasn't that the agency was squeamish, or too noble. They'd done that sort of thing before. Even if current weaponry didn't do much to the worms, which it didn't, they could have developed something that did. The agency had done that before too.

Marshall also thought a way could have been found to live with the beasts. Floating cities were one idea. Perhaps energy fields the worms couldn't penetrate could have been built. He wondered if some sort of vibrations could have been produced to influence the nervous systems of the worms, surely the agency had something like that, to either drive them away or turn them passive. Surely some solution could have been found.

Yet again, the agency had done that sort of thing many, many times before.

But no.

The Apocalypse Amelioration Agency told people to flee. They packed everyone up again, and took them right back to where they'd just left.

Now, if someone was paying attention they might have seen a problem with this plan. Marshall certainly had a certain amount of hesitation when it was announced. After all, earth had been destroyed when the sun became a red giant. That was why they were all on the new planet to begin with, right?

Funny thing, apparently the agency hadn't totally given up on the earth. They'd kept trying to fix the sun after the evacuation. Perhaps they sent everybody off in case it didn't end up working, or in case they couldn't do it in time.

But, they had. The sun's chain reaction was reversed by blasting in a load of new fission material, turning back the clock for a good long while. The earth escaped unscathed, and the agency had told no one. Perhaps they were embarrassed they'd gone to such extremes unnecessarily by packing everyone up, or maybe they were saving earth in their back pocket for an emergency.

That could have been why they hadn't tried too hard with the worms. Why bother if they could go home? Whether that figured into the agency's calculations or not, what happened is what happened.

The people were loaded back onto the freighters. Another couple months of their lives were wasted in space flight, though it wasn't like most of them made good use of time anyway. People returned to earth and to their homes. For the most part, life on earth took right up where it had left off.

Bonnie had been quiet during the return flight, much more so than the first one. Marshall hadn't wanted to pry.

He thought maybe she needed some time to process things, some time without speaking. It didn't seem like anything was wrong, but he didn't know for sure. Whatever it was went on inside her. But Marshall was a little scared to make whatever it was come out. Bonnie could be volatile, reasonable as she was about it.

They were reassigned back to his old apartment though it had been expanded a fraction as there were two of them now. Marshall went back to work soldering communication units and Bonnie went back to the food distributorship. Despite her sudden taciturn bent, they did well together.

Then the climate changed.

Polar regions warmed and tropical regions cooled. Oceans levels raised, or lowered, or something. Reports varied and it was difficult to be certain. The agency satellites went haywire trying to keep up. Food production was decimated and famines came round. It was chaos once more.

And then, everything was fixed. The agency finally got the weather satellites to stabilize the situation, and the weather returned to normal.

Twelve o'clock and all was well.

"Another one down," Marshall quipped to Bonnie when they got the news.

"Aaaagggghh," she screamed. She grabbed him by the collar and shook. Marshall noted she really was quite strong, no matter how small her build. "How can you keep taking this? It's insane. It never stops."

Marshall worried when the snap would come, quiet as she had been. Now it finally happened though, he was strangely calm. She wasn't mad at him, she was just pissed in general. "I—"

"—that's it," she said. "We're going to do something. We're going to do it now."

Interlude

Please pardon my rambling here, if you happen to read this. I sincerely doubt anything in these pages is of actual value, or that my scribblings aren't going to wander around for a while. Frankly, this is a tremendous waste of time.

Still, I've been advised it is necessary to step away from the office now and again. One can become too focused, thinking only of the job every hour of every day. It supposedly isn't good for identity. The role apparently can overcome one, the individual drowned in the collective one.

I can see that, to some extent. Don't misunderstand I debate that point. However, there is little time for stepping away. Some item always needs attention, courses of action, and consequences to be pondered. It's unending.

When is one supposed to step away? What is one to do about all what should have been done in the interim? Won't there be even more work waiting when one picks back up again, due to the period of absence?

These arguments were not refuted. However though the validity of my point was admitted, the need for a space, despite the consequences, was reiterated. The claim was advanced that performance after a breather would be superior to working through the lost time, thus justifying.

I wasn't certain I agreed, but my agreement was not sought.

Then the point was raised regarding what this step away should consist of. What else was there besides the work to be done? Perhaps that itself was a sign I hadn't been switching away enough previously. Maybe it's already too late.

"Keep a journal of your thoughts," was the prescription I was given. "Make them non-work thoughts. Have it be whatever goes on in your head when you aren't thinking about work, not an excuse to further develop issues you need to solve instead of actually taking a rest," they said.

You can see how well that's going.

There is a certain danger in sitting down to record one's thoughts, I think. One may actually find one has none. That's an unpleasant thing to learn about one's self and I think most people should avoid it, better to remain in the dark.

Sure, people think they have thoughts. If they had time to finally focus on them and put them down somehow, that would surely be a wondrous thing. But, do they? Do they really? Is that what they would find when they finally try, or would they turn out to be empty, all that crowding in their brains apparently only having been the illusion of thought, perhaps merely a substitute for it?

Sometimes it turns out what they actually had was other people's thoughts. That's embarrassing. All that time you thought you were thinking things, only it turns out it was recycled thoughts from someone else.

So there you are, all set to work out what's in your head, and all you've got is some gripes about the fact you're being forced to do it and some rehashing to waste time on.

How unpleasant. How embarrassing, even if no one reads it.

As you must have imagined by now, this is what I'm currently facing.

Thus, I'll have to ask you to indulge me some. I'm going to plagiarize and complain. That might be all I get around to, finding nothing further in the well beyond that. However, trying to hold out some kind of hope, perhaps I've got something of my own underneath. Maybe I'll have to dump all the rest out in order to be able to sift through and find it.

Anyway, in the beginning, God created the heavens and the earth.

Light and dark, land and sky, however that was different from the heavens and the earth, plants, stars, animals, woman and man. At least, we think God was the one. Reports have him issuing a lot of enabling orders without any real specific mention of actual creation, but that's what we have to work with.

Of course, it was good.

But, it must not have been completely good, because there seemed to be a second beginning. The two are kind of glossed into one, but it looks like there were two at one point. Thus, the above we shall call the first beginning. The below we'll call the second beginning.

In the second beginning, a lot of stuff from the first beginning also happened. As above, so below. However, though plants and animals had already been created, God created them over again. He also made man again, despite the fact it had already been done. He made both man and woman the first time, but he only did one the second time and then remade one from the other.

The second beginning was a lot longer than the first beginning. There was a moral in it. People were told not to do something and, of course, they immediately did this and were responsible for all their own suffering in life.

Details. Characters. Drama. Then murder, boats, and drunkenness.

Things got more complicated from there.

Maybe that's why there were first and second beginnings. Perhaps the first was merely a warm-up. Since the second was going to be such a big production, maybe a dress rehearsal was necessary. Maybe more than one, and we don't know about the others, it's hard to say.

Now, God didn't appear to have been involved in the third beginning. Maybe he or she sat that one out. Details are a bit scant and there isn't any mention of him/her.

In the third beginning, the world formed on the back of a giant turtle. We only know a turtle and the world forming on its back, its shell. Not sure what it formed from, or where the turtle came from, but there it was. The world. On the back of a giant turtle.

Of course, one couldn't have the turtle floating around in the emptiness of the void. No sir! That turtle would fall. Have no fear though; the turtle was riding on the back of another turtle. Doesn't that make everything okay?

No, we have no idea where that second turtle came from either. Nor do we know why the first turtle was standing on the second. There is also the question of why neither turtle tried to eat the forming world, but we don't know the answer to that either.

What we do know is you're likely wondering what the second turtle was standing on. After all, we told you the first turtle was standing on the back of the second, and the world formed on the back of the first. Aren't you curious about what that second turtle was standing on? Of course, you are.

The second turtle was standing on the back of a third turtle.

See how easy that was? Orderly, symmetrical. Well thought out, properly documented and explained.

Of course, the third turtle was standing on the back of a fourth turtle. The fourth was standing on the back of a fifth turtle. The fifth was standing on the back of a sixth turtle. And the sixth? Why, the sixth was standing on the back of a seventh turtle.

Hopefully you haven't tuned out yet.

But, what about the seventh turtle? Surely you're demanding I explain what the seventh turtle was standing on. I've bothered to explain about the others. Why not this one? Surely that seventh was standing on something.

To borrow a phrase though, I have to tell you, No dice, man. It's turtles all the way down. So ends the third beginning.

The fourth beginning was a bit different. By different, I mean compared to the other three beginnings. There was definitely no God. No turtles either.

In the fourth beginning, there was a large bang. All matter in existence was compressed down to a singularity and then it exploded. Stuff hurled everywhere, continually expanding. As the junk flew, some of it started spinning. Out of that spinning, mass settled. Out came stars and planets and other coalesced debris. Where things settled out, they started rotating around each other.

On some of the settled junk, there were chemical reactions. Lightning, gas clouds, liquids, amino acids, all kinds of things were happening. Life happened. Single cells. Single celled organisms became more complex and turned into multicellular organisms, though some were still single celled. Life morphed and changed. It diversified. There were many different living things: plants, and animals, and bacteria, and fungi.

Conditions changed from time to time. Life evolved. For some reason, one thing mutated into another. Sometimes the mutation caught on, but other times it did not. Occasionally, one set of things with a certain set of characteristics suited to current conditions thrived and reproduced while another set of things with less suitable characteristics went the way of the dinosaurs. One example was, in fact, the dinosaurs.

This went on for a while.

This was the fourth beginning.

Now, the fourth beginning was highly intricate and efficient. I'm not describing it particularly well, but it was. No one can fault the fourth beginning for that. However, it was widely recognized the fourth beginning was the most boring of all the beginnings. For that accusation, I will provide no defense.

I should admit, by widely recognized I mean this is how I feel about the matter. I don't know what anyone else thinks about it.

Sure, there's the whole majesty of nature thing about it. I'll admit that. Still, it's pretty clinical, no magic. Maybe there is no magic, and I've certainly never seen any, but shouldn't beginnings have at least a little?

The fifth beginning is secret. I can't tell you a single thing about it, don't ask. I have no knowledge of such a beginning. Even if I had such knowledge, I would not be disposed to discuss such a beginning at this time. The same goes for the sixth beginning.

Now, the seventh beginning was just plain wacky. Seriously, if you thought there was anything odd about beginnings one through four, or five or six even though I didn't tell you about them, you clearly aren't familiar with beginning seven.

Anyway, a bunch of penguins were living in a ceramic bowl of cold spaghetti noodles. There was no tomato sauce because it didn't exist yet, but that was okay. As the spaghetti was cold, moisture condensed upon it. This kept the spaghetti from sticking, or from sticking to the penguins, or the bowl. It also kept the penguins from sticking to the bowl, and from sticking to each other.

As I mentioned, tomato sauce did not exist yet. You should realize since this was a beginning, the moisture didn't either. Neither did the bowl. I think you can guess about the penguins. How could there be penguins if nothing existed yet?

This bunch of nonexistent penguins was living in a nonexistent ceramic bowl of cold, nonexistent spaghetti noodles moist with nonexistent moisture. Obviously, this was not a pleasant situation. Nonexistent penguins were not meant to live in a nonexistent bowl of nonexistent spaghetti. They'd have been more suited to living at a nonexistent South Pole. I mean, obviously.

Something had to change.

Given the penguins were dissatisfied, they created everything.

That was the seventh beginning.

Frankly, I think the seventh beginning can be explained by the fact the first six, by definition, since there was a seventh, had not gone well. A lot of things had been tried, but clearly something else was needed.

However, beginning seven apparently wasn't it either.

This brings us to beginning number eight.

Part II: Birds and Snakes, an Aeroplane

While you live, your troubles are many, poor Jerusalem.
To conquer death, you only have to die.
You only have to die.

-"Poor Jerusalem," *Jesus Christ Superstar*

Seasons don't fear the reaper
Nor do the wind, the sun or the rain
We can be like they are
Come on baby
Don't fear the reaper
Baby take my hand

-"Don't Fear the Reaper," Blue Oyster Cult

Well there's a punk in the alley and he's looking for a fight
There's an Arab on the corner buying everything in sight
There's a mother in the ghetto with another mouth to feed
Seems that everywhere you look today there's misery and greed
I guess you know the Earth is gonna crash into the sun
But that's no reason why we shouldn't have a little fun
So if you think it's scary, if it's more than you can take
Just blow out the candles and have a piece of cake
Happy birthday.

-"Happy Birthday," Weird Al Yankovic

Chapter One

Now turned out to be a flexible term. After Bonnie's snap, Marshall thought something was going to happen. Bonnie was going to do something or tell him to do something. The moment seemed action-oriented.

However, nothing. After she screamed and demanded action, she didn't announce any immediate plans.

She attacked no one and she did not approach the agency. She didn't try to persuade anyone of anything. She went quiet and it was as if the outburst hadn't happened. Marshall was tempted to pretend it hadn't. Though he wasn't sure why, it seemed like an incredibly bad idea.

Marshall thought he needed to keep his eyes open.

Bonnie seemed quieter than before. It wasn't as if she couldn't talk though Marshall wondered at times. It was more that she wouldn't. He was concerned, but not exactly scared. Regardless, it was best to be alert.

She would answer if he asked a question. She would use as few words as possible, often one, but she would answer. Closed ended questions were easier. A few words could be a complete answer. Open ended ones, ones requiring multiple strings of thoughts and explanations, usually received an I don't know. Things he said to her that were not questions provoked no verbal response at all.

She never asked him any questions, or spoke at any other time.

However, despite having no evidence one way or another, he didn't believe she was merely broken. Nor did he believe she was angry with him. She wasn't shut down. She was thinking. Plotting. He couldn't point to anything specific, but he knew. He'd be told when he needed to know.

Until then, Marshall decided to be patient. He was good at that. Well, he was at least good at resigning himself to things he couldn't change. The apocalypses were proof enough of that. Hopefully he wouldn't have to wait for the end of the apocalypses before Bonnie started talking again.

Bonnie still went to work. Marshall did as well, thinking she would have an easier time at his job with not talking than hers. The assembly line was merely soldering, no words required. How did she work a food distributorship silently? Maybe they had her unload boxes in the back, stock shelves, something not involving waiting on customers. Marshall didn't know.

However they handled it, she kept going.

Marshall and Bonnie kept going out as well. Walks, picnics, all kinds of things. She wasn't physically distant either, only verbally. Marshall would have preferred more communication, but perhaps she felt they did enough in other ways. It was hard for Marshall to say for sure without being able to ask for an explanation.

It was actually another apocalypse, or at least the threat of one, that broke her out of the shell.

"Citizens." Malcolm's voice boomed once again.

They'd been pulled out of bed in the middle of the night so they could go outside to see the broadcast. Everyone had, those who'd been sleeping were uniformly bleary-eyed. Communication units weren't utilized, no messages, no alerts. There were late night poundings on house doors. The agency apparently wanted everyone watching live.

"Citizens, our lives are yet again threatened. If we hope to survive, we must pull together. The help of each citizen is necessary; each must do his or her part."

People whimpered to themselves in the crowd. It wasn't everyone, but the mumbling was fairly widespread. They weren't sure what to think. The agency always took care of things. People didn't pitch in, help out. It scared them to think they would have a responsible hand in their own destinies, and they didn't seem particularly happy about the idea.

"A cosmic phenomenon has come to our attention. There is a radiation cloud drifting its way through space. Tremendous in size, it spans nearly half the length of our solar system. Though not composed of any discernible particles or mass, a variety of disturbing wavelengths emanate from it. Most are extremely harmful to our kind of life."

Marshall looked at Bonnie, but she hadn't reacted to the news. She seemed aware, fully awake, and looked back at him with recognition, but she was not visibly upset. No screaming or shaking. No grimacing or jaw clenching. No smiling either. Or laughter. Nothing. She merely watched the broadcast and appeared interested in what was happening.

"It is not clear how the cloud moves, since it seems to drift through the cosmos independent of rotations and gravitational fields. It is also not apparent what processes go on inside to produce the emanations. What is clear is where it is going. Our solar system is directly in its line of travel."

Pause.

"There is little need to be dramatic as much of familiar space is also in that path. We just happen to be right in the middle."

People were all still listening, but the mood of the crowd wasn't particularly dark. Instead of worrying about the impending apocalypse for once, they seemed more concerned about what they were going to be expected to do. They probably wondered if it was going to be hard. They waited to hear that part. Marshall supposed he shouldn't be surprised, presuming that was what they were actually thinking.

He bet it was.

"Our normal shielding fields are insufficient to protect us," Malcolm explained. "We will simply be too deep in the cloud for too long. We have every reason to believe the environment itself will be unharmed once exposure is over. However, we are immediately concerned about prolonged human contact with the kind of wavelengths we have detected."

Marshall wondered why they didn't merely load everyone into the ships again. No need to colonize elsewhere, but they could at least take a trip out of the way for a while. A cruise.

It was almost as if the agency didn't want the apocalypses to get repetitive, dull.

That was ridiculous. There had to be a reason why the ships weren't used. Perhaps there wasn't a safe region reachable in time. Also, Marshall reminded himself Malcolm hadn't gotten to the solution yet. He hadn't said they weren't using the ships.

"We will need to go underground."

A collective intake of breath ran through the crowd, which seemed silly to Marshall. It was a dramatic announcement, but utterly without specifics regarding what it meant as of yet. They were jumping the emotional reaction gun again, but that's what people always did. Too early, or too late, as if they weren't reacting but were acting and missing their cues. Reactions never made sense. They were malformed due to unhealthy mental living conditions.

"This will be a gigantic construction operation. We will need sappers to guide the excavator machines to carve out our planned shelters. We will need builders to create the walls within which we will wait for the cloud to pass. Food and water, air, heating, and cooling, everything must be entirely self-contained and sealed. We will require the talents and skills of all citizens for a project of this size."

Marshall noticed one reaction in particular, Bonnie's.

Everyone else took in the instructions, their emotional climax already finished. Bonnie however, had a glint in her eye and a crooked smile that made Marshall nervous. It was not a smile boding well. Then, as if she didn't want her expression seen, her face went impassive again, mildly interested.

"For those of you who do not think you have talents or skills," Malcolm went on, "do not be concerned." He smiled. "We will find tasks for you. Everyone will be useful."

The crowd recovered well from their shock at actually being asked to help save themselves. They were standing up straight, their chests puffed out with pride. They were not the usual sheep bleating in fear over the coming wolf. No, they were intent worker ants patiently waiting to be told how they could save the colony.

There wasn't much difference as Marshall saw it. The emotional tone wasn't the same, but the character of the crowd seemed interchangeable to him.

Actually, Marshall wondered if it wasn't a good idea to get people involved in those sorts of things. For one thing, it would distract them from the drama in which they normally engaged during apocalypses. Children were dangerous when not occupied. Besides that, contributing seemed to make them feel as if they weren't merely at the whims of fate, that they had some kind of control. It struck Marshall as better than the way things were normally done.

Eventually, the sky went dark and people were told to return to their homes. Organization of the shelters, who would do what where and when, would begin in the morning. The Apocalypse Amelioration Agency would, of course, manage everything. Individuals merely needed to do as told. There was time for construction of the shelters before the cloud and earth intersected, but not an endless amount. Work needed to begin immediately.

Marshall was not shocked to be assigned to an assembly related task. That was how events usually developed. However, he was a bit startled to learn Bonnie had been as well.

How would she react? Would she refuse?

Though the matter had not been explicitly discussed, he had the idea she was unwilling to do what she felt was her real work under existing circumstances. It was something he simply understood.

Would she give in? What would other people, or the agency, do if she didn't do as told?

His reaction to the additional discovery she had actually requested the assignment was downright shock.

Sure, it was possible the crisis had stirred some responsible aspect of her and she decided to put aside her personal feelings. She could have seen her skills were needed and decided she couldn't rightfully refuse, not when everyone's cooperation was legitimately needed for survival. It was possible, it really was.

Then again, it was also possible Marshall could transform into a purple cow at will using undiscovered shape changing powers he possessed and simply wasn't aware of because he'd never tried to do it before.

Neither was particularly likely.

Marshall was uncomfortably certain this was part of some plan about which she had not yet seen fit to inform him. There had to be a reason, and that reason was a hidden one. The possibility of this other scenario was about as likely as the occurrence of another apocalypse.

In other words, it was a virtual guarantee.

It might have been thought, if Marshall had explained his reasoning to anyone, that he was paranoid. He had no specific evidence of a plan of any kind. However, not only had Bonnie requested an assembly assignment, she had requested a specific task. It was a task that needed to be performed by two assembly workers. The other worker? Bonnie requested Marshall.

As mentioned above, the possibility of a Bonnie plot was almost completely certain. And though he was nervous, he had no choice but to go along with it. He hadn't learned anything yet that would make him think he should oppose it, and he thought he had to trust Bonnie and hope for the best . . . hope when the virtual certainty occurred it was something he could live with.

The actual task was relatively simple, but geographically dispersed. The cavernous underground shelters were to be built in hundreds of locations around the globe. Each one was to have its own water-processing center. It was a relatively small device, considering the number of people it would support, but vital. Water supply failure was one of the quickest ways to die, absent a violent death. Bonnie and Marshall were to install the controller modules for the processing centers at each of the various shelters.

Every single one.

A skiffer was provided for their official use. As soon as a shelter's water-processing center was constructed by the appropriate respective personnel, Bonnie and Marshall were dispatched a notification. A relatively short skiffer flight later, they installed the controller module together.

Bonnie still hadn't mentioned the plan.

She had started speaking again, almost as if she'd never stopped. She frightened Marshall a little by her sudden flip back. She answered his questions. She asked questions of her own. She joked, she chatted, she shot the breeze. However, she didn't say a word about what they were up to.

The controllers were the primary functioning component of the water-processing centers. Since the shelters were to be completely contained, no new water would be able to come in. Instead, each water-processing center collected all waste, whether human excretion, leftover food, hygiene water, or whatever, and extracted pure water back out of it. The process was performed utilizing atomic separation and recombination, as opposed to filters that would eventually jam. An endless supply of clean water was possible from a single decent sized storage tank.

Marshall noted Bonnie made some modifications to each of the controller modules prior to installation.

Bonnie said nothing about the modification. She didn't say a word about it during any of their installations. When he asked about it after he got up the courage to do so, she smiled and insisted there was no modification. He quickly ascertained what it would do, but swallowed and decided to see where she was going with it. He stayed with his decision to trust Bonnie.

No one else seemed to notice the modification.

He did not expect she was going to do the same thing to the shelter they were eventually going to be sealed within. He had no reason for thinking she would not be completely thorough, but he ignored that lack. He kept telling himself she wasn't going to, or she had a side plan for keeping them unaffected.

She didn't.

No, eventually the human denizens of earth were all locked into their respective shelters, Bonnie and Marshall included. Soon, pretty soon since it started on the first day the hatch doors were sealed, people began drinking the recycled water.

That's when they got the runs.

Not just Bonnie and Marshall. Almost every human being on the planet, only almost because some would seem to get better before succumbing again, had the runs. Millions spent months curled up in corners, writhing in pain and abdominal cramping. This says nothing of the discomfort and embarrassment, though everyone was pretty much going through the exact same thing at the exact same time.

No one was seriously hurt or killed by the situation, but a great number of people had a fairly nasty time of things until the cloud passed and it was safe to come out. In fact, it was accurate to say everyone had kind of a shitty time.

The modification Bonnie made caused the water-processing centers to not produce pure water. The output was actually a mixture of fresh water and a small amount of potent but relatively safe laxative. Resources were on hand to keep citizens safely hydrated, but not to end their distress. Nor could the controller modules be modified until after the cloud passed, had anyone besides Marshall and Bonnie known what the problem was.

As Marshall endured his pain, he figured there had been no way Bonnie could have pulled it off and kept them out of it. They had to suffer as well if it was going to happen. He knew he'd ignored that concept beforehand, perhaps so he didn't think about what he was about to undergo any sooner than necessary.

And, to an extent, Bonnie's plan had been a success. For reasons utterly unrelated to any potential mortality or actual life danger, people suffered the most unpleasant apocalypse to date. No one wanted to ever go through anything like it ever again. Surely that had been Bonnie's scheme.

But, she had inadvertently saved humanity.

As it later came out, the shelters had not been thoroughly shielded enough. Radiation from the cloud, minute amounts, managed to penetrate the shelters. Everyone was exposed. The exposure was minute, but later analysis revealed it would have easily been enough to kill them all.

Each and every man, woman, and child.

The Apocalypse Amelioration Agency was far from perfect.

Then add the laxative into the equation.

Horrible though it was on a daily basis, it flushed small amounts of radiation from people's systems. Levels built up more slowly than they would have otherwise. As a result, people lived.

Bonnie's prank had saved the human race.

Marshall was apprehensive about going home when it was all over. The cloud gone and radiation levels dissipated.

He knew Bonnie was going to be pissed.

Chapter Two

It was stupid.

Marshall shook his head. There was no other way to describe it.

Stupid.

Well, there were probably many other ways to describe the situation, actually. Some of them were probably more accurate than stupid. Still, Marshall stuck to it, it was apt.

He'd just gotten home from work when the sky lit up with Malcolm. He was at his old job. They were both back at their old jobs. No one ever mentioned the laxative modification, he didn't know if anyone looked into it enough to discover what happened, but the controller module tack had only been temporary. Since it was over, they went back to what they'd been doing before.

Marshall went to work on the line. He went home. Right outside his building, he watched and listened to the details of the current apocalypse.

He didn't see Bonnie anywhere outside. There was the usual crowd, but she hadn't been in it. It was her day off, so maybe she hadn't left the apartment. Or, perhaps she'd gone out for some project and had not yet returned.

There wasn't anything notable in her absence, he didn't think. She would get details some other way. It wasn't like an apocalypse could often go off and leave one out of it entirely, though some did happen quickly enough to be gone before one became aware. There was no need to worry about those apocalypses though.

Bonnie lounged on the bed, flipping through a book on religious mania she'd found during a scavenging mission, when Marshall came into the apartment.

"Hey," she said cheerily.

"Hey. Did you hear?" He nodded to her communication unit sitting on the floor. "About this one?"

She shook her head, smiling. "Nah. I heard the alert and figured something was going on, but didn't feel like checking. I'm relaxing, why spoil it? You'll give me the specifics. Besides," she said, pointing at her communication unit, "it's all the way over there. I would have had to get up."

"Ice nine."

"What?"

"That's what's going on outside, the apocalypse. Someone developed water with a different molecular arrangement so it stays frozen at higher temperatures. Up to one hundred and fifty degrees Fahrenheit. It turns normal when boiled, but it converts old water if you introduce it." Marshall said. He sighed angrily.

"Could cause a few problems," she admitted, a puzzled expression on her face.

"Yeah, the oceans and rivers are currently solid," Marshall continued. "The fish are all probably dead. The agency rationed water until the situation gets fixed and sealed the water treatment systems away from external sources. Travel to anywhere near the frozen stuff is prohibited."

"So?" Bonnie yawned. "What's bugging you? Were you planning a trip or something?"

"No." Marshall threw up his hands. "It's Ice Nine."

Bonnie frowned. "Okay . . . you're going to have to explain. I'm not getting something here."

"Ice Nine was from an old novel, Cat's Cradle by some guy named Kurt Vonnegut. I had to read it back in college. It's exactly the same thing. The whole apocalypse is right out of a book."

Bonnie smirked. "Maybe the guy who came up with it was a fan, read it, and decided to see if it could be done. Guess it could."

"It doesn't matter," Marshall groaned, "but can't we have original apocalypses? If we have to keep suffering these things, does it all have to be compounded by being a rerun? It's like whatever's in charge ran out of ideas."

"And that's new?" Bonnie waved a hand dismissively. "We've had dozens of apocalypse repeats. Even some that weren't exactly the same were pretty similar."

"It's just so boring," Marshall growled. "Seriously, I don't get how people can still care. Even if they might die, there's no meaning in it anymore. I mean, come on . . . what's next? Novels? Where can it go from there?"

Bonnie sat up, grinning a familiar grin. It should have made him nervous, it usually did. He was too pissed to get nervous though. This time it kind of excited him.

"Want to do something about it? At least make a statement?"

He nodded. He did want to do something. Without knowing what Bonnie had in mind. He doubted it would do anything. Still, he didn't seem to care right then if it did. Something needed to be done, something more than swallowing it all and smiling politely.

Bonnie hopped off the bed and got started. She grabbed old sets of clothes and tore them up. Not shredding them into strips or anything, more making them tastefully holey. Getting dirt from outside, where it could still be found, and rubbing it in. The leftover fragments from the holes she turned to ash, though she didn't scorch the outfits themselves.

The fire part actually wasn't easy. There weren't a whole lot of working heating elements anymore. Matches and lighters only existed as rumors. Cooking was primarily done with fields. However, Bonnie had saved some of the first generation oxygen burners from the other planet. Cracking the case open, she got access to the arc flame. Then she did her incineration on one of the many paved areas outside.

"Dress up?" Marshall asked amidst the flurry of preparation.

Bonnie nodded to him and held out his scruffed outfit. He put it on and she did the same with hers. The point wasn't clear yet, but Marshall started to see it taking shape.

Bonnie found some light scrap metal lying around the apartment and fashioned them a pair of large signs. After locating a couple marking sticks, she wrote THE END IS NAY upon the signs. She handed one sign to Marshall and shoved the marking sticks into his pocket.

Before they left the apartment, she smeared ash all over their faces. "Don't get it in your mouth," she advised. "This stuff is synthetic and probably isn't good to eat." Then they walked out into the streets looking like a pair of old time prophets. Signs held high.

Marshall thought the idea was more amusing than anything else, but he went along with it willingly. He didn't voice any concerns once he figured out what she was doing. It was little more than silly fun, but he figured that was enough. If nothing else, it was better than sitting around the apartment stewing, which is what he realized he would otherwise have done.

Outside was the usual chaos. People copulated, unconcerned about who their partner(s) was/were, certain it was their final moment. Smoking. Drinking. Drugs. Looting. Rioting. Destruction. All the normal end of the world shtick. Some people simply screamed. Some ran in terror from the others. In short, the usual.

Marshall reflected as they walked in their rags, with their faces blackened, and their prophecy held out to the world, that the mess was even less appropriate this time. Though life was imperiled, the danger was not particularly immediate. Nothing was coming for people, capable of striking at any time. Instead, it was literally slow moving. Death could take a while to arrive though the ocean had frozen in a flash. Given such, why freak out as if the end was imminent?

Perhaps people were getting it all out of the way, efficiently ahead of any actual doom part of the apocalypse. He doubted they planned that well though, or at all. It was more likely they didn't have any other way to act. It was an apocalypse. They were conditioned. It was time for a freak out.

Bonnie led Marshall though the streets, stopping to mark messages on walls with the marking sticks as they passed. Like the signs, the scrawls all read THE END IS NAY. She wasn't regular about it, or methodical, but the action was frequent. Often, whenever there was a good bit of empty wall.

Marshall did as she did, but not at the exact same times or the exact same places.

Eventually, she got bored. No one noticed the wall messages, or seemed to. If they did, no one confronted Bonnie and Marshall about them. Regardless, no one heeded the messages though

Marshall hadn't expected anyone to. It was just something to do, but the novelty wore off. Something else was needed.

Marshall followed Bonnie right into the mass of people. Some parted for them. Sometimes she shoved open a path. She used her sign to clear people aside.

"This is not the end," Bonnie shouted. "The end is not upon us."

"It's okay if you haven't repented," Marshall joined in. "There's still time."

People didn't seem particularly surprised. Some noticed, but kept right on doing what they'd been doing. Gorging, screwing, breaking, panicking, they looked up and then went back to their activities. Marshall thought they seemed to find renewed gusto, almost as if their freaking out had gotten boring and a doomsayer provided a recharge. Perhaps the non-doom message didn't matter. The image of the doomsayer was enough.

Nothing changed.

"The end is nay." Bonnie kept shouting.

Marshall leaped atop a heap of recently broken junk. "People," he bellowed, "the end of the world isn't remotely close. You have all of your lives to live. Nothing is going to be different."

Bonnie chimed in, "If the moon turns as black as sackcloth and the moon runs red as blood, they'll be back to normal in a day or two."

Marshall went on, "However bad things seem, life goes on."

Bonnie ran over and thrust her sign at a man copulating with two women. "You, sir. Have you made your peace with the maker? Are you ready to be called home?"

The man looked up, surprised enough he stopped what he was doing. The women, however, continued. They took little notice of his halted participation.

"What? Yes."

Bonnie threw open her arms joyously. "Well, why? There is no reason. You'll have to do it again when the world really ends, because it isn't going to now."

The man turned away, noticing the copulation had continued and there was no longer room for him. Unconcerned, he looked for another opening and found a different pile soon enough. His previous pile didn't appear to miss him.

Bonnie and Marshall shouted a while longer. Marshall jumped down from the junk heap and they wandered around some more.

Sometimes they shouted. Other times they marched and brandished the signs. Once in a while, they stopped and wrote anti-apocalyptic messages. The crowd around took no notice.

Eventually, Marshall and Bonnie got bored and went home.

They took off the rags, washed off the ash, and put on clean clothes. The signs were tossed into a corner. Bonnie picked up her book again, settling back to relax for the evening.

"Huh," Marshall commented, looking at his communication unit. "It's over already."

"Yeah? What'd they do?"

"Someone found yet another new form of water with the exact freezing properties of the old. The new-new stuff turned all the new stuff back to normal on contact. Everything's liquid again, where it's supposed to be at least, and the Apocalypse Amelioration Agency is going to restock fish from hatcheries they've been maintaining."

"That's good," she commented, already reading and only half paying attention.

Nothing had been accomplished, Marshall admitted, but at least this time they hadn't been part of it. Since things couldn't be fixed, screwing around wasn't bad, necessarily. He wondered if he was only rationalizing, but immediately put it out of his mind.

"They should call it water ten," he remarked.

Chapter Three

"Nobody's going to buy these costumes," Marshall told Bonnie. "You don't know what these things look like, but this definitely can't be it. There's no way this will work."

"No one else knows what they look like either," she shot back. "The broadcast didn't include any images. Besides, we wouldn't want to really look like them, we need to look dumber. That's the whole point, creating doubt. People just have to think this is what one of them looks like."

Giant monster lizards.

The radiation cloud hadn't exactly had no effect on the environment. Marshall doubted anyone thought it would have none. Everything has some kind of effect. One apocalypse, and/or its solution, tended to spawn another. Sometimes not, but most often it did. Even if people had escaped an apocalypse unharmed, or unharmed enough until cancer levels, or kidney failures, or some such thing's statistics had time to develop, it was a matter of waiting to see if there was another shoe to drop.

The only time you were sure was when there was, and you knew that only when you heard it hit.

A shoe dropped this time, as Marshall and Bonnie learned, while looking again up at the sky. Lizards, Malcolm told them. Lizards mutated because of the cloud exposure.

It was an iguana breed, one previously common in a number of parts of the world, despite all the previous apocalypses. After this particular apocalypse, it became a great deal more common.

The mutant lizards were capable of asexual reproduction. They reproduced at a frightening rate, dividing and spreading all over the place. Quickly, they covered most of the planet. And, the lizard replication showed no signs of slowing. If anything, due to the increasing number of lizards capable of replication, reproduction increased exponentially.

Lizards all around.

"It doesn't work that way," Marshall complained to Bonnie as they watched. "Radiation causes sickness and death. It doesn't morph."

"Oh yeah," Bonnie snorted, "because everything else that's happened followed regular rules. Nothing untoward happened before this."

The monsters increased dramatically in both size and intelligence along with their increased and altered breeding ability. They were a bit larger than men, at least so far, and they were incredibly strong and resilient. They healed at tremendous rates, when any way had been found to even slightly damage them. Little success had been found trying to do that much.

Super-powered-giant-monster-replicating-lizards. SPGMRLs.

"It's right out of some old comic book. Radiation doesn't work like that."

"I know. Shut up, I'm trying to hear."

More problematic, more than their explosive reproduction, which was itself a severe problem, was the fact they acquired a taste for human flesh.

It was unknown if this was a side effect of the exposure. As the reptiles had previously only grown to a foot or two long, man had not been a dietary possibility. Or perhaps humans may simply not have been within reach. Now that they were, the creatures might have proceeded with gusto, making up for lost time. Perhaps that's why they were going after man and nothing else.

Then again, maybe it was the radiation. Maybe it warped their original desires and tastes as well as their bodies. Perhaps it made them crave human flesh at the same time it provided the ability to get it.

However, that part didn't matter much. The human-hunting state of affairs, absent some finding causation was bound up in how to stop it, was the thing to worry over as opposed to what brought it about. The reasons were for academic debate later, once there were no more SPGMRLs trying to eat people.

Citizens were told to stay indoors whenever possible, preferably in multistory buildings off of the ground floor. For the moment, hunting only happened in the streets. As of yet, the SPGMRLs had not figured out how to break inside. When staying indoors was not possible, citizens were encouraged to travel by heavy vehicle or stick to open areas.

At least according to current observations, the SPGMRLs could not run as fast as a human.

Like the zombies, Marshall reflected, the biggest danger was in letting oneself get cornered. Not surprising then the transport pods had been entirely shut down for the time being. It seemed like they'd almost been designed for trapping people into corners.

Again Marshall wondered about use of the ships.

Why not run? It was a nightmare to get so many people into them, and the ships were a giant corner until they took off. However, they were better protected than most buildings. People would only be targets while waiting outside to get in. Ways could probably be found around that as well, like sealed tunnels leading inside. Then, once loaded, they could take off until a SPGMRL solution had been found.

That wasn't done though. Instead, they were told to avoid the monsters, stay inside as much as they could. In the meantime, solutions were being discussed.

Lacking anything better to do, people went home. Some still went out and about, but they did it quickly. No SPGMRL sightings had been reported in Marshall and Bonnie's city to date, but people were being cautious.

Marshall and Bonnie went home as well, but not for lack of a better option. Actually, it was in further of something better. At least, it was in Bonnie's opinion. She had a plan.

"Everyone is going to avoid those things," She said. "Then the monsters will be gone and nothing will change. What we need to do is make people think the lizards don't need to be avoided. Then they won't and they'll get eaten. That'd be a change."

"And how are we going to do that?"

She smiled. "By becoming lizards people don't need to avoid. Encourage a sense of complacency, and let the lizards punish those who fall for it. Natural selection."

Marshall pondered. "How many do you think you could reach? Twenty? Thirty? Is it worth the bother?"

Bonnie shrugged. "Got a better idea?"

Marshall had to admit he did not. As such, he followed along and assisted Bonnie in her preparations.

Lizard suits needed to be built. They needed to be maneuverable, yet durable. They needed to be made from things Marshall and Bonnie could get. There was no sense spending weeks obtaining suitable parts only to find the Apocalypse Amelioration Agency had already exterminated the horrid things.

Maneuverable seemed more important than durable. Marshall and Bonnie didn't want the suits to fall apart, ruining the scam, but they were under no illusions any actual protection would be provided. The suits would help neither against a mob suddenly finding the backbone with which to fight back, nor against agency soldiers trying out new weapons, which would almost certainly be dramatically effective. Certainly not against actual SPGMRL attacks.

Bonnie made frames out of lightweight scrap metal piping. Marshall didn't know why she had it, but decided it wasn't important enough right then to ask. She had a lot of things she'd picked up in the course of scavenging for different projects. The joints were flex conduit and hardening polyresin.

Of course, decently strong and flexible though the frames turned out to be, they didn't look very lizard-like. In fact, they looked more like cybernetic power armor, though ricketier. Perhaps an amateur version. The frames needed lizard skins.

Bonnie already planned for that though, cannibalizing old polymer/metal hybrid thermal emergency blankets. She insisted they were perfect, already stretchy and scale-like with various shades of light semi-irridescent green. She felt that suggested radioactive in a way naïve people would expect.

Pincher hands, webbed feet, big black insect eyes, and a single horn protruding from the forehead. Stretched out over the frame,

Marshall admitted it looked vaguely reptilian. However, he didn't think it looked as convincing as Bonnie did. Perhaps it looked a bit cartoonish.

Then again, it was her design and her plan. Maybe it was just more like what she thought the SPGMRLs would look like than what he thought they would.

That was when they had the debate about suit verisimilitude mentioned earlier. Marshall didn't end up agreeing, but he was already committed to the plan. It was a bit late for quibbling, unless he wanted to junk the whole thing, which Bonnie pointed out. But then Bonnie would be disappointed and they wouldn't do anything.

Marshall tried to resign himself to the suits.

Still, the mood created was one of comedy, not terror. Even draped over the furniture as they worked, no animating human pilot inside, he could see how they would come across. They'd be anthropomorphic lizard puppets from a children's show, not fearsome SPGMRLs that ate people. Marshall felt ridiculous and he hadn't put his on yet.

"Look," Bonnie told him, apparently sensing his reluctance, "we're supposed to look goofy. Remember? We don't only want to behave as if we aren't threats; we want to look that way too. People react best to messages presented in multiple ways and we'll be less effective if we acted dumb but looked scary."

Marshall again had no real argument to make though he wasn't feeling completely good about it. Bonnie gave up trying to convince him and just put the plan into action.

It was decided not to merely put the suits on and walk out of the apartment. Lizards coming out of a door like people might have ruined the illusion a bit. And, on the off chance people were stupid enough for it not to, they decided it best not to have mobs or soldiers storming their home. Instead, they took the suits out in carry packs, dressed normally, and hid behind a building to put them on.

Then they were lizard monsters. SPGMRLs.

Though they intended to present a comic face, and run from any trouble they found, Bonnie decided not to go out defenseless. She brought the shotgun and had Marshall bring one of the kinetic rifles. It was doubtful either would be great against SPGMRLs, certainly having already been tried by the agency, but they didn't have other weapons lying around. They'd have to try it if there was no other choice and hope it would help. Besides, either would certainly work on an angry mob of citizens.

Bonnie mounted them in a leg of each of their suits, determining they needed to be able to get at them but that SPGMRLs carrying weapons was a bit over the top. All Bonnie and Marshall had to do was rip off some fake skin in case of emergency.

Once suited, Bonnie and Marshall began wandering the streets. At first, their pretend lizard movements didn't jibe. Bonnie thought the SPGMRLs would move in slow, almost oozing ways when not currently attacking. Marshall, on the other hand thought they'd dart around every which way like fleas. A divided approach was agreed to be unconvincing. After more debate, they settled on a hybrid of the two approaches. Neither felt it mattered much, as long as they were both doing the same thing.

Then they were on the hunt.

Of course, they'd somewhat overlooked the fact people had been told to stay indoors when possible. They lizard-marched around, but had difficulty finding anyone to mess with. It wasn't much good with only the two of them out there in lizard suits.

Luckily, they eventually happened upon a couple trying to break into a shuttered food distributorship. The couple hadn't gotten far and the store was locked up pretty tight. Really, they were simply beating the lock repeatedly with a metal bar. Obviously, these were not major talents.

"Hiiisss," Marshall and Bonnie spat as they came running up on the pair, waving their arms in what they felt was a lizardish fashion. "Hiiisssssssss."

The woman of the couple screamed though the man would have apparently joined in if he hadn't been too terrified to do so. The couple hadn't been paying any attention, no thought of SPGMRL dangers. Marshall and Bonnie surprised them completely.

They pretended to snatch at the couple with their pincher hands. It was tough to get the people to react, easier to actually attack them, but that would have frustrated the purpose. The couple seemed too stunned to defend themselves.

Finally, Marshall got the idea to grope the woman's breast. Then the couple reacted, the woman shrieked and the man raised the metal bar to swing. Marshall and Bonnie pretended to become frightened, running away and hissing. Unfortunately, the couple ran also.

"Well, that could have gone better," Marshall commented as they ducked into an alley.

"Why? They got the better of us pretty easily."

"Yeah, but we probably scared them as much as we made them confident."

"Call it a wash then," Bonnie conceded.

A hiss sounded from the other end of the alley. Neither of them had made it.

"Shit," Bonnie mumbled.

A lizard the size of a small horse slithered into the road ahead of them. A SPGMRL. A real one.

It was less hominid than they'd imagined, on all fours with its belly dragging on the ground. It definitely had an upper torso though, clearly defined muscularly from its lower half. Hugely muscular. It was clearly on its way to man-like mobility.

The head was more elongated though with a definite snout. There were also many more teeth than they had supposed. Bonnie and Marshall could see that much with the beast's mouth still closed. The talons looked tremendously sharp, marking the pavement with scratches as the behemoth moved.

The skin was much more gray, and almost appeared to crackle and illuminate irregularly with electricity. Saliva dripped from the thing's mouth and sizzled on the road. Their conception had been very wrong.

"Run." Bonnie ordered.

Unfortunately, they heard a similar hiss from the mouth of the alley directly behind them. Another SPGMRL moved in, they were blocked.

Bonnie and Marshall tried to run to one side, but the one in front easily copied the move, as did the one behind. The beasts did it with only the upper half of their bodies, blocking as much of the road as possible. Bonnie and Marshall were definitely being hunted. Running didn't look like much of an option.

Marshall ripped the kinetic rifle out of the leg of his suit at the same time Bonnie unloaded on the one in front with the shotgun. Unlike the creamed corn, the shot didn't even seem to break the skin.

Marshall let go with the kinetic rifle. There was a shimmer, and then two SPGMRLs instead of one stood in front of them. Kinetic rifle blasts apparently triggered reproduction.

There were now three SPGMRLs in the alley.

"Shit," Bonnie yelled again.

The SPGMRLs crept in closer, but they began to mysteriously slow. A bitter chill tore through the air. The temperature dropped almost instantaneously and snow fell.

"Blizzard apocalypse," Marshall mumbled.

The SPGMRLs struggled to approach, but appeared to be in slow motion. They halted and settled to the ground like collapsing air domes. Their eyes closed. The beasts slumbered, apparently still cold-blooded.

"Now," Bonnie shouted, vaulting over one of the sleeping monstrosities. Marshall quickly followed.

As they ran through the snow back toward the apartment, they tore at the suits. Long before they reached home, only the pipe frames remained. Back in the alley, the shotgun and kinetic rifle were already buried in a foot of accumulating snow.

Chapter Four

It wasn't any good. None of it, none of it was any good.

Marshall trudged through the snow, thick furs wrapped tightly around him. The cold was biting. His boots punctured a tough ice shell on the surface and sunk into the deep drifts below, only stopping when enough compacted to support his weight. Crunch, crumple. Crunch, crumple. Snow blew everywhere in the darkness. Every which way. The wind whistled.

Well, they weren't actually furs. There weren't enough fur-bearing animals available. They were synthetic, but they looked real enough. Probably for whatever psychological effect, or maybe there was something in nature's design that fought against cold. Regardless, the synthetics were warm.

In those kind of temperatures, warm was necessary. Vital.

He liked Bonnie. He liked being with her. Did he love her? He wasn't sure. He didn't know. If it was simply something one knew, then he knew. But, what did he know? If love was something one couldn't know until having been in it, then how would one who hadn't been in love differentiate it from any of the lesser yet similar states?

That didn't help either.

Marshall trudged home to their snow hut after working at the emergency heating device factory. He'd felt like thinking, so he hadn't gone straight home. He made a trip to the temporary food distribution center to pick up their rations, lugging them home in his carry pack though Bonnie worked there and could easily have brought them home the next day.

That hadn't been enough time for thinking though. His thoughts still hadn't settled. He walked for a while and looked around, mainly at snow since there wasn't much else to look at.

Thinking.

The city, much of the planet in fact, had been covered in a strangling blanket of snow. The stuff accumulated to the point most buildings were below people's feet. Things were pulled out as the snow all came down, but most returning home would have to wait for whatever melt was coming. Until then, people lived atop it all. Temporary homes floated above the real ones.

The Apocalypse Amelioration Agency gave out emergency shelter units, but they were only supposed to be a base. Snow huts had to be built around the tent-like things made of heat generating polymer. That and the emergency heating devices kept people relatively safe from the cold, but caused a bit of melt here and there. Thus, the snow huts were somewhat of an ongoing process, at least until the ice age was over.

Screwing around with apocalypses had been fun for Marshall, at first. It was a change from going along with them like all the other cows. But, in the end, it wasn't much different. Even with the minor disruptions Marshall and Bonnie managed to provide, things pretty much went their normal course. Marshall had no illusions the disruptions had been anything but minor. He sincerely doubted any future plans would approach the level of major.

Honestly, he wasn't sure if he wanted them to.

Would Bonnie keep scheming? Would Marshall keep going along? It was getting old. Did she see that? He wondered.

Making a statement seemed like a good idea, but was it such a fine thing when it wasn't made to anyone? No one listened, that was clear. And, statement or no, no one listening meant they were only babbling to themselves. As fun, though traumatic, as what they'd been doing was, it felt a lot like raving in a corner.

Regardless of whatever was said about statements, they were only amusing themselves. The apocalypses had been boring and Marshall and Bonnie kept themselves occupied by messing around. It passed time, but it was six of one and a half dozen the other. It was a cliché, boring in its own way.

It wasn't enough.

Worse, him and Bonnie didn't seem to be enough for him.

Marshall paused on a ridge. Snow swirled, but the sky itself was clear and he could see the full moon. He looked at it for a while out there in the cold. The moon, the ever-present moon. Not exactly unchanging, waxing and waning as it did, but certainly not there one moment and gone the next.

At least, he hoped not. Weirder shit had happened.

Still, beautiful as it was in its dependable constancy, it was not a growing thing. There was no moving forward. Change was in the past, the moon was the moon was the moon. At least it had its chance to become.

He and Bonnie didn't have a chance to become.

Technically, they were married already. At least, there didn't seem to be any further requirement to fulfill for a marriage beyond what they'd already satisfied. It was pretty basic. Formal licenses and things were fazed out as luxuries, things people found too hard to accomplish amidst everything else. Marshall and Bonnie spent time together. Why did it feel to Marshall like it was still surface?

What more could he need? It wasn't like they were waiting for kids and couldn't have them because the world was fucked. It was, but neither seemed to feel the need to reproduce. They could, people did, but neither of them were particularly nurturing. That wasn't what was missing.

And it wasn't as if they didn't connect on a significant level, deeper than they did with anyone else. They hadn't even tried to talk to others about the apocalypses, they were the only ones and they told each other at least mostly everything. Maybe they didn't all the time, but sometimes they didn't need to. Some things were already known.

Marshall was the one who'd stopped talking much this time. He needed to grasp what was going on and it was hard to talk and comprehend at the same time. He hadn't withdrawn or anything, he merely hadn't been saying a lot since the snow started falling.

Maybe winter made him turn inward, hibernate, though it wasn't really winter. It had actually been the lizards. One apocalypse caused another apocalypse that in turn ended the first apocalypse. Satellites.

Not that the lizards had gotten into the sky. They hadn't mutated to the point of wings, at least not functional ones. Even if they had, space would likely have been beyond their reach. At least for a while. They couldn't have gotten to the weather control satellites themselves without ships. Certainly, no one was going to drive them.

However, it was a little known fact that the weather control satellites were still controlled by ground stations. It was a remnant of an older technology, an artifact no one apparently thought to update.

For some reason, lizards got into the ground stations. No one knew why. The things hadn't even been manned anymore. It couldn't have been for food. Maybe it was the warmth. Maybe the electromagnetic field attracted the things. It was hard to say, and pointless to speculate since it had happened anyway.

At first a few nested in one of the stations. Then those few multiplied. You can imagine what happened then. If you can't, just understand all the ground stations went out. Corrosive saliva, gnawed wires, overheated components, acidic droppings and urine. Cut off from control, the satellites spun off into deep space or reentered the atmosphere and burned to tiny flakes of ash.

The results were pretty similar.

Immediately, the planet was plunged into the global ice age. The thought was the climate had been controlled for so long it swung wild to balance once the satellite interference ceased. It'd swing back eventually. In the meantime though, people were cold.

Of course, there probably wouldn't be time for a normal settling of the climate. The Apocalypse Amelioration Agency would launch new satellites. Those would definitely not be ground station controlled.

The lizards were gone. They were pretty easy targets once the cold hit, and they went into a stasis state.

But, back to Bonnie and Marshall. Marshall reflected this was always the way, always the problem. Apocalypses got in the way between him and her.

Granted, an apocalypse brought them together. They might not have met otherwise. And, an apocalypse had brought them closer. Gotten them married. As of yet, apocalypses hadn't actually separated them though one or more still could. That wasn't the issue though.

Likely, they'd hang around each other until one decided to leave or died. Perhaps related to an apocalypse, or it'd at least be enough like one if it occurred. Barring such a thing, actual or in effect, they could grow old together. That wasn't it.

So what was it?

Marshall had trouble setting it all out precisely. Maybe that was one reason he hadn't mentioned it to Bonnie yet. He admitted to himself there could be more to it.

Marshall checked the snow packed around their emergency shelter unit. It was fine, but it was so nice out, dark and quiet, that he spent a while packing on more. It looks like a damned igloo, he thought. With the fake furs, that made him into sort of an Eskimo. Or Inuit? Marshall couldn't remember, since either was long gone.

Maybe a person couldn't form attachments when surrounded perpetually by the end. Bonnie and Marshall couldn't go anywhere. There was no life to build, just lives they could live in the same place, connecting where possible. That's all there was, there could be no more.

And, good as it was, it wasn't enough.

Marshall sighed. He couldn't stay out there forever. Not that he wanted to, but he didn't want to go inside either. With neither option seeming satisfactory, he decided on the warmer one. He went inside the hut.

The main room was empty. Not empty of stuff, empty of Bonnie. He didn't see her anywhere. She should have been home, not having to work that day, and the place wasn't exactly big.

"Bonnie?"

No response. The place was quiet. He looked around in what semi-counted as other rooms. She definitely wasn't there. At first, he only wondered. Then however, he realized her furs were still piled in a corner.

He grabbed Bonnie's furs and ran back outside. He scanned the area intently. What he found, missed on the way in, half-filled as they were from snowfall, was a set of footprints. They led off in the opposite direction from the one in which he'd come. Marshall figured as much. If he'd gone by her, he'd have noticed a girl with no coat out in the cold. Even wrapped in one's own thoughts, it would have demanded attention.

Hurrying, he followed the prints. Whatever his thoughts, he was going. Everything else could be sorted out later. He definitely didn't want what it looked like.

Bonnie was simply standing when he came upon her, dressed in black shorts and a tank top. Underclothes really. She stood there, turned away from him, and watched the moon as he'd done. She didn't seem to notice his approach.

He ran in front of her. Her eyes were open, but they were dim. Her skin was white, tinged blue. Her face was blank, as if asleep.

"Bonnie. What are you doing? Do you want to kill yourself?"

"No," she replied weakly, "I wasn't doing that."

Her voice was quiet. Slow. Marshall was reminded of the lizards just before they'd gone to sleep. Bonnie was frozen, in more ways than one. She didn't look frostbit yet though, but surely dangerously cold.

"How long have you been out here? Why don't you have a coat?"

"I don't?" she responded. She blinked. It was the first time she'd blinked since he'd been watching. "Maybe I didn't want a coat. I don't think."

He stopped asking questions. There'd be time later, if the answers mattered. He wrapped her in the furs he had dragged with him and guided her back.

Inside, he parked her right next to the emergency heater device. He kept her wrapped up and turned the device on as high as it would go. Carefully, he tried to warm her core first. Then, he moved on to her extremities. He remembered that being the right thing to do for hypothermia. He couldn't be sure, but there was no time to get help.

Given the current situation, as with most situations, there was no one to call.

She didn't fight. Or protest. When he wrapped her up, she accepted it. When he walked her to the hut, she went as long as he pushed, and in whatever direction. As he warmed her, she seemed as if it was a perfectly normal thing. If she'd done it intentionally, she showed no sign as he worked to counteract the cold.

"How's that?" he asked.

"Warm," she responded.

Eventually, the blue tinge faded from her skin. Though pale, she wasn't as pale as she'd been outside. Her face reddened a little, flushed from the heat coming off the device. Her eyes focused. She woke from her trance.

She looked around the snow hut, taking in where she was. She looked at Marshal, taking him in. He didn't speak, just watched her nervously, making sure she was okay.

"I picked up the rations," he finally said, wanting to test how responsive she was.

She nodded. Then, after a moment, she said: "We need to talk."

He nodded, suddenly sure what she was going to say. It wasn't going to be she was leaving, either of the ways that could be meant. He knew that much. It was going to be something else. And it was going to be big.

Chapter Five

Marshall and Bonnie walked around the pond in the park. It was warm, the snow long gone. The newly launched weather control satellites were obviously working, but the climate had started returning to normal anyway. The ice age apocalypse had been relatively brief.

No more emergency shelter units. No more emergency heater devices. No more snow huts, or furs, or rations. Bonnie and Marshall had moved back to the apartment.

"So . . . you want to talk through it again," Bonnie said.

"I didn't think we'd finished the last time," Marshall replied. "Or the time before."

It was the same park from the zombie apocalypse though there were no corpses anymore. As a result, it was pleasant. Not even a rotting arm or toe had been left behind. All had been disposed of, errant bodies returned to the graves from whence they came by the Apocalypse Amelioration Agency. The park seemed actually more beautiful than it had been before, more lush and green. Perhaps the corpses had acted as fertilizer somewhat before removal. Or, perhaps they hadn't been removed and had been completely absorbed, feeding the soil. Regardless, though the park was more pleasant than before, Marshall and Bonnie were not having a picnic.

They'd talked the night in the snow hut as Bonnie recovered from exposure. She'd come right out with it. They talked, and then they talked the next day. They hashed it out quite a few times since then. It seemed to be their only topic of conversation. Bonnie acted as if there was nothing to discuss, it just was what it was. Marshall couldn't let it be that simple.

"You want to kill everybody," Marshall exclaimed. "I think that merits a bit of discussion."

"Does it?" she looked at him. "What is there to say? Yes or no seems to cover it pretty well, Lunk."

Marshall grunted. He realized afterward the grunt only reinforced the whole Lunk thing. It had felt like such a satisfying way to respond though, possessing a certain dignity.

What frightened Marshall most, on a number of levels, was deep down he agreed with her. No other solution seemed possible, and they'd both been thinking it. Bonnie had simply been pushed a little farther, been a little sicker of it all. She was the one who actually gave voice to it.

Still, it wasn't something one immediately jumped to, no matter how right it felt. Killing all of humanity? That needed to be considered. Fully. There had to be a certainty there were absolutely, absolutely no other options. Even before deciding. Even before actually trying to figure out implementation. There had to be that. It was big deal. It had to be.

"Look," Bonnie said, "I'll go through it again if you need me to. I just don't see what we haven't talked about already."

"I'd like that." He waited. If he was going to make this kind of decision, then she was damn well going to be the one putting forth some effort. She had to convince him, even if he was already convinced.

He wasn't ready to be as convinced as she was.

"It keeps happening," she finally went on. "It won't stop on its own. Ever."

She glanced at him, but he looked straight ahead. They kept walking, another circuit around the pond. They'd walked quite a few laps already.

"We can't change what causes them, especially since it is so many different things. Going against the flow was nice for a change, but what did it get us? It brought us here, and we've been here before. No better."

Marshall shrugged. "It's a nice day to be here. There aren't any zombies."

"For now. Anyway, don't be facetious," she retorted. "Disruption was a first step, a prelude. It can only lead one place. There was only ever one place though we didn't think about it."

"Destroying the world?"

"Well . . . yes," she quietly admitted. "I don't like it either, but what else? What else? It's the only way to be sure there's never another apocalypse . . . a successful one, finally. If the world actually ends, it can't end again."

"People could die off and then the planet could explode later," he countered.

"Sure," she agreed, "but that wouldn't be the same thing, would it? Destruction happens in the universe. Planetoid collisions, supernovas, whatever. But that isn't something consciously waiting for some final moment to mark and take stock of its existence. That's life, not an apocalypse."

Marshall nodded.

"Apocalypses need something, humans, who are going to consider it such," she concluded.

Marshall picked up a flat rock. He winged it at the pond, skipping it across the surface. After seven skips, the rock embedded in the mud bank of the island.

"You know I'm right."

"That doesn't mean I want to die," Marshall protested. "That doesn't mean I want to kill everybody. I don't. I want other things."

"So do I. It doesn't change anything."

They were silent for a while, looking around. The park was empty of other people. Marshall wondered why no one else ever seemed to come. Maybe the corpses had rotted there long enough people never forgot the stench, but he remembered people hadn't come there much before. He also realized he was only thinking about it to avoid thinking about killing everyone.

"Doesn't it seem odd to you?"

"What? Deciding to commit mass murder? Of course. How do you think I feel?"

"No." Marshall shook his head. "That's not what I meant. Trying to cause the Apocalypse. That's what it'd be. If ever there was a correct use of the term, it would be then . . . if it worked."

"It would," she said. "The only time it ever should be used. It's meant to be a one-shot word."

"And we'd be causing it," he continued. "We hate apocalypses and here we'd be starting one. Intentionally. Doesn't that bother you? At least as much as the idea of mass murder?"

She grimaced. "It would be different. Stopping it would make up for that, and it would be real for once."

Marshall, tired of walking or, at least, tired of both mentally and physically going around in circles, sat down. He rested his back against a tree. Bonnie sat down next to him, resting her head on his chest. She draped one arm over him.

"I don't want to die," he said again.

"I don't want to either," she said, "but I'm willing to."

"How would we even do it?" he argued half-heartedly. It was so academic, so devil's advocate. He couldn't stop himself. "Neither of us have a doomsday machine. We wouldn't have the first idea, or ability, to build one. Isn't it all talk if we can't act?"

She ran a hand across his chest. "I don't know, but I know we have to. We have to come up with something. Maybe it'll work, maybe not. But, if it doesn't, we'll probably be killed and won't have to worry anymore. Then the point will be moot."

Marshall threw up a hand. He would have thrown up both, but Bonnie was on top of the other and he didn't want to disturb her. No reason to when he could still get his point across. "Why not kill ourselves then? I'm not saying to, but why not? It'd be easier and we wouldn't have to care anymore. And we wouldn't have killed all those people. It's got some plusses."

Bonnie shook her head. "We'd still know it was going to keep on. At the final moment, we'd know. At least if we try and fuck up then there's a chance we can die thinking it might stop."

"Or maybe not."

"True, maybe we'll know we fucked it up."

Marshall thought she was going to keep talking, come up with some counter point, but she didn't. She acknowledged the possibility and let it drop. As if that was all that needed to be said, as if what they were talking about wasn't so epically important it deserved to be debated from all angles, as if all points didn't need to be resolved favorably before going forward. She just agreed and shrugged.

As if it didn't matter.

"But—"

Bonnie put her hand lightly over his mouth. "Let me tell you something, Lunk. Okay?"

He nodded.

"When I was little, I used to have one of those powered bikes. You know, the ones that made all the motor noises though they were a silent electric operation and had pedals you could pump but didn't do anything. Remember those?"

"I remember."

"Good," she continued, "I used to ride it everywhere. It wasn't any different than taking the transport pods, but I insisted on riding it wherever I went. School, home, you name it. Mine was black and had fake flames painted down the sides."

"I had one too. Mine was red. Every kid probably had one back then."

"Probably. Anyway, one day it stopped working. I took the engine apart and laid all the pieces out on my bedroom floor. There was a loose looking wire by some burn marks. It looked like the solder had contained impurities and it eventually got too hot and sizzled, popping loose."

Marshall looked down at her hand on his chest. She looked at the sky. "What'd you do?"

"I re-soldered it and put the bike back together. I was six or so, but it wasn't too hard. Anyway, I took my power bike right out for a ride then. Just down to the store and back, a quick trip to make sure it worked right."

"Okay." Marshall started to wonder what the point was.

"Outside the store, there was this little dog tied up. People still had dogs back then. I remember imagining the dog had been left there and its owner was never coming back, a poor little dog. There was no reason to think it, and I didn't really. I imagined it though."

"Did you take the dog?"

"No, I left it there. I'm sure its owner was right inside and came back out to get it pretty quick. I merely rode my bike home."

Marshall sat up. Bonnie lifted her head off his chest to let him move.

"I'm sorry," he said, "but this is bugging me. Where is this going?"

Bonnie smiled. "Nowhere, Lunk. I'm only talking . . . just like we've been doing."

Marshall swallowed.

"We can talk and talk and talk. Go around in the same circles trying to reach a destination we both know doesn't exist. You want to do that? Fine, I'll do it as long as you want. Just don't think it's anything else. There's nowhere else to go, nothing you can answer that we haven't already. At some point, you have to make your decision. But, I'll wait."

She put her hand on his chest again and pressed him down, back against the tree. He resisted at first, but then he let go and went with it. She put her head back down on his chest. For a while, he merely watched her head rise and fall as he breathed.

"Okay," he finally said. "If we find a way, I'm in. I'll destroy the world."

Chapter Six

Marshall was awake. It was early in the morning, still a ways from time to get up, but not far enough to go back to sleep. He remained in bed. Bonnie was next to him, still sleeping. He looked out into the dark.

His brain had been working while he slept. Remembering, considering, working things out. Then, arriving at a conclusion, it must have decided to wake him up so he could be informed. All he knew was he was suddenly awake and there it was. This confused him for a moment, like walking into the middle of a conversation concerning you but you have no idea what came before, or where it came from. Even more confusing to have it happen in your own head.

"Bonnie," he said. He shook her shoulder lightly.

She started awake. "Mmm? What?"

"I have an idea," he said somberly.

"Just one?" she mumbled. "What is it?"

He chewed on his lower lip. "One may be all I want, since it's a way to end the world. I woke up and it was there."

She sat up and turned on the light. "If it's for the final apocalypse then one is fine. What is it?"

Marshall looked up at the ceiling. "For some reason, I remembered this drive I took back when I was still an undergrad, back when people still had personal cars. It was a while ago."

"Okay," she prodded.

"I was working on an improved bit-less drill design for a team project and I needed a specific ore type to test it on. Obviously I wasn't going to find any ore in the city, but some old survey maps showed promising formations out in quadrant twelve."

"A little ways out of town," she quipped, "but not exactly a road trip."

"Right, but you know how unused quadrant twelve is for the most part. I'd never gone there, it's mostly dirt roads. Hard to find your way around without a navigation system, which weren't common at the time."

He reached over and grabbed water from a stand near the bed. He paused to take a drink.

"I was following a route marked 735-alpha, which was supposed to lead to those formations. But, there were a bunch of barricades across the road. They were pretty run down looking, and I couldn't see any reason they were there, so I went around them. I had no choice. I couldn't figure out another route from the survey maps. It was either that or turn around and give up. That's when I ran into the ghost town."

"Ghost town?"

"An empty, abandoned town," Marshall explained.

"I know the term," she snapped, "but I don't know of any in quadrant twelve. I've been out there collecting before."

"I'll get to it," he assured her. "Let me finish. Anyway, I pulled up into this old town square. There weren't any towns on the survey maps, so I was pretty sure I was lost."

"Probably were, Lunk."

"That's what I thought at first, sitting there with the maps spread out on the car hood, but something was off. I noticed weird little things."

"Like?"

"Well, the place looked old. Real old. There was a statue of a guy with one of those guns people used to have to pack gunpowder into. Only, I realized it was made of polymer instead of old bronze. I saw a log cabin, but the logs had been fixed to a frame and hung, like a sheet."

"It only looked old."

"Yeah, purposefully, but it definitely wasn't. Things looked good from a ways away, like it was left over from the before times and simply hadn't fallen down yet, but up close you could tell."

"Strange."

"That was when a guy in a personnel skiffer landed and asked what I was doing. Came out of nowhere, but quick, as if he'd been watching and saw the exact moment I drove up. I said where I was trying to go and he told me I was on 735-gamma instead. He gave me directions, friendly enough, but he stood there long enough to watch me go."

"Still sounds reasonable." Bonnie yawned. Marshall couldn't tell if it was because she was half awake or if he was losing her interest.

"But it wasn't. Those directions were malicious and got me completely lost. It took me hours to get back to a road I could find the city from again. I never did find those formations."

"So? Some people can't give directions."

Marshall shook his head. "No, they were purposefully bad. Calculated. It led me in a total maze. He had to have wanted to make sure I wouldn't find my way back again. I figured out later I could only have been on 735-alpha. The guy lied."

Bonnie's eyes narrowed. "Why?"

"I couldn't figure it out for a while, and it bugged me. Eventually, I went back looking. I think I found the spot again, but there was no town there anymore. Instead, there was miles and miles of metal fencing, all topped with razor wire. Multiple rows of fence and Apocalypse Amelioration Agency soldiers all over the place. It had to have gone on forever, but they'd managed to fence it all off. All flat ground. Whatever had been the town had been snatched up and spirited away."

Bonnie held up a hand. "Wait a minute. You aren't trying to get me back for the power bike story, are you? This goes somewhere? If you say there was a little dog tied to the fence then I'm not listening anymore."

"It goes somewhere, hang on." Marshall took another drink of water. "Anyway, I started thinking. Back in the really old days, they used to hide nuclear missile silos under fake towns. That was before the scans could see right through the ground, but it used to obfuscate them. Explain the heat signatures and other activity. That had to have been what it was. It's the only thing that explains a fake town. Maybe the Apocalypse Amelioration Agency took it down because it didn't blur scans anymore and only made people curious, but they still had the area locked down. Probably for safety, getting rid of an entire missile wouldn't have been easy."

Bonnie reflected. "I know that compound. That I did come across while collecting from abandoned installations out there. I didn't poke around too close with so many soldiers there though."

"Exactly. They were guarding something. I bet the missile is still there, one of the big ones designed to take out fifty different cities anywhere in the world. Otherwise, why so much security?"

Bonnie shook her head. "They couldn't have left it. Even with that kind of precaution, why not get rid of it? Given what always happens?"

Marshall shrugged. "But then why guard? Maybe they had nowhere else to put it, or no time to bother. Maybe they were saving it to use for combatting some other apocalypse. I don't know, but why hang around if it was gone?"

Bonnie didn't seem to have an answer.

"It might still be there. We might be able to launch it. It's even possible the old nuke response networks, the old defense response grids automated in case of surprise attacks, are still in place too. We could wipe it all away with one single launch."

Bonnie looked skeptical.

"And even if the grids aren't up anymore, fifty warheads, presuming it is one of the big ones would easily be enough."

"Don't you think the agency would have prepared?" she rubbed her chin. "Nukes? We've had a nuclear apocalypse before, and it was handled."

"Sure," Marshall admitted. "One lone nut blew off a small bomb, but there's never been a big nuclear strike. There haven't even been individual countries for ages now, why would they be prepared for it? They deal with what they face at the time, not what might come down the road. That's why stuff is probably still lying around. They can't work on everything all the time."

Bonnie bit the end of her tongue, chewing lightly. Marshall waited for official approval as she considered things.

"We'd still have to get past security," Bonnie said. "Got a plan?"

"Actually, I do." Marshall smirked, in spite of how he felt about what they were discussing, pleased to be a step ahead of Bonnie for once. It didn't happen often and he relished it. "Nothing."

Bonnie frowned. "Run that by me again, Lunk."

"They had me on emergency snow removal when the thaw started, for a short time between when the emergency heater devices weren't necessary any longer and my reassignment to the communication unit factory. The freight skiffers we used to suck up snow left in the streets to prevent later flooding needed somewhere to dump. Guess where they picked?"

"It better have been quadrant twelve or you are telling a power bike story."

"It was. We didn't get too close, but I could see the fence. There wasn't anybody there. The soldiers were all gone. The whole place looked abandoned."

"So your idea about something having to still be there if they were still guarding falls down," she argued. "They don't guard anymore so they must have deactivated whatever had been there."

Marshall rubbed his chin. "I don't think so. In the middle of a snow apocalypse? I bet they needed people elsewhere too badly, and it wasn't enough of a concern since it was already in the middle of nowhere and protected by all the fencing. Plenty of people got reassigned during the snow. Why not soldiers? Maybe it wasn't enough of a worry when it was over to put everybody back in place. We'd have to get through the fences and such, but we could get in."

Bonnie stood up. She rummaged through her piles of junk. Pulling out a small-handled object with two black metal prongs coming off of it. She set it on the bed.

"What are you doing?"

"Getting equipment together," she explained. "Come on. If we're doing it, we're doing it. Get the carry bags."

"Now?"

"Any reason to wait? We've got to hurry. The world's about to end."

Marshall felt a little useless as Bonnie pulled everything together. It was his idea, but she was the one who seemed to know what they'd need or, at least, what they hoped to. They were her tools anyway. Marshall merely packed. He consoled himself it was at least his idea. Without him there would have been nothing to pack for.

As much as anything about it could be considered consoling.

Marshall hoped anew, despite not wanting to be hoping, the ICBM would still be there. Now they were actually going, he had fresh doubts.

Still, he could worry about that later.

"Where are we going to get survey maps?" Marshall asked, trying to be helpful. "We'll need something. I won't be able to find it again otherwise. It was an accident the first time, and when we buzzed it in the freight skiffer. I couldn't repeat it."

"I can," Bonnie responded. "As long as it's the place I'm thinking of, I could find it blind. I've been all over that quadrant. You can even get close by transport pod, within about ten miles or so. You walk that far?"

Marshall nodded. He had to be good for at least some part of his plan. What a terrible thing to want to be good at, he thought. Regardless, he wanted to contribute to the big event. He wondered if it meant he was as bad as everyone else, as idiotic. Wasn't that what all the apocalypses were for them? Something making them important in a way they worried they'd never be? He might have only been fooling himself he was different.

Was Bonnie?

He startled out of his thoughts when Bonnie tossed one of the carry packs at him. He caught it though it was heavy. Metal clanged inside.

"Let's go, Lunk. Hopefully time is running out." She grimaced.

He slowly put the carry pack on his back. They were going to end the world.

People appeared normal as they walked to the transport pod. They were doing what they always did when there wasn't an apocalypse. People were going to work, going home, doing whatever they did with their lives. They looked happy enough.

It was still early morning, so not too many people were in the streets. There were some though. Early risers or night shifters just returning home, Marshall supposed. People. Ordinary people.

The day was nice. Marshall could tell though it wasn't fully light yet. Not an apocalypse in the sky, he thought, and then realized it didn't make any sense. What a shame a world like this had to end. Then he remembered another apocalypse was likely right around the corner anyway. It usually was.

He redoubled his walking speed. They were going to end the world.

Marshall followed Bonnie to the transport pods. No one looked at them strangely. They should have. He reminded himself no one knew what they were up to. No one had any reason to look, to stop them. Still, it seemed like they should have been able to feel it. Intuit it. No one did. Marshall and Bonnie were just two more people on the street. Nameless. Faceless. They got in a transport pod and rode for a while.

They got off when they got to the terminus on that portion of the line. Fewer people were about, even though it was later in the day. They were in the outskirts of civilization. Fewer people lived there.

They wandered off the roads and out into the empty places beyond the city.

Marshall wasn't in the best of shape, but he didn't think he was too bad. He walked a lot. Still, he wasn't prepared for an extended forced march. Even Bonnie appeared to have trouble after a while. She didn't talk about it, just kept walking. He did the same.

They could see the fence long before they came upon it. Rows and rows of the stuff. It looked new, interlocking metal with razor coils atop. Intimidating, but there were no soldiers. No patrols. Marshall and Bonnie still hadn't seen anyone when they got right up to it.

"Think it's powered?" Marshall asked. "Or alarmed?"

Bonnie took out her communication unit and held it close. "No fields. There'd be some kind of field if anything was active. I guess it's only a fence. Anyway, now or never."

She took out the handled object with two black metal prongs. As she twisted something, the prongs glowed an electric blue. Marshall could smell burning plastic. "Plasma bar," she remarked.

He nodded. Whatever that was.

When the prongs got brighter, Bonnie touched them to the fence. The metal melted away like running water. Bonnie cut a large hole in the fencing and they walked through. She did that with each fence they came to.

After a good number of fences, they found themselves in a flat grass-covered clearing. It was large with a giant metal disc in the center, as wide across as a city block. There were seams in it, but no apparent way to open the thing. Bonnie tried the plasma bar, but it cut in a little ways and stopped. The metal was too thick.

"What now?"

"There?" Bonnie pointed. A hatch sat over in a corner of the clearing near a fence.

They walked over. There was a small metal wheel attached. Putting some effort into it together, they got it to move. Soon the hatch popped open, and revealed a downward proceeding tunnel. Bonnie pulled out a pair of head-mounted illuminators and they descended.

They didn't speak.

The tunnel led down into an underground tower. There were various rooms, filled with manuals and powered-off equipment. There were planning rooms, monitoring rooms, barracks. They found another tunnel leading to another tower, and then another tunnel.

At the end of the second tunnel, they felt a cool breeze. The illuminators didn't shine in far, but they could tell the room was cavernous. It felt like the bottom of a giant well.

They were in the main silo.

Bonnie stopped by an immense switch mechanism labeled Main Portal. They could read that even in the dimness from the poor light of the illuminators. She reached for it and stopped. "Ready to see how good your plan was, Lunk?"

He nodded and she threw the switch.

Amazingly, machinery responded. The noise was deafening, clanging of actuators the size of mountains. Millions of turning gears. Light flooded in as they watched the ceiling above them crack and separate. The giant metal disc of the heavens above split and slid away into unknown pockets. Soon, all they could see was the sky.

Actually, it took a few moments for that to happen. At first, all they saw was brightness. They'd been in the underground for so long even restricted sunlight was too much. However, after a moment, their eyes adjusted. They could see again. They could look around.

The silo was empty. There was no missile.

They stood, staring, for a little while as if they merely couldn't see the missile yet because they were still dark-blind. Blind to the ICBM and nothing else. Surely it would pop into view any moment and they'd see it as clearly as they currently saw the empty silo.

But it wouldn't. The missile wasn't there.

"So, Lunk," Bonnie finally said, obviously trying to mask disappointment. "I don't suppose you have any other ideas?"

Chapter Seven

Marshall didn't respond. What could he say? There wasn't a missile.

However, there were some things they didn't expect to find at the bottom of a missile silo. A large terminal setup, much bigger than any system access point they'd ever seen, certainly larger than their communication units. Trunks. Storage cabinets. A tub, partially open on one side, as large as a normal room.

In fact, a room appeared to be set up in it. Vid equipment, connected to the terminal setup, pointed into the mock room of the tub. None of it looked like it belonged in a missile silo.

"What is this, Lunk?" Bonnie asked, walking over to the terminal setup. "This place is old, but the equipment is pretty new. They didn't have this stuff in the missile days, particularly an access point like this."

Marshall walked over and scanned the mock room. It looked familiar. He'd seen it before. He knew it. But, where?

"I don't know." He shook his head.

Bonnie tapped at one of the screens on the terminal setup. It came to life, glowing. Marshall couldn't see the screen's data from where he was, but he could tell the setup was active on the system. Bonnie activated other screens and began typing occasionally on them, accessing something.

The vid equipment was odd too, heavy grade stuff. He could figure out what the recording equipment was, pointed at the room. The cue board was easily identifiable as well, a neat electromagnetic toy you could write on as many times as you needed and then tap to clear. That was all recognizable though more serious and more complex than the versions he'd seen before. It was all hooked into some kind of spotlight thing, aimed at the aperture above, big as their whole apartment.

It had one giant lens instead of a lamp unit, nearly as big across as whatever it was itself. Black and cut like a gemstone. It reflected his image in a skewed fashion when he looked into it, but it also seemed to suck in some of the ambient light. He found himself thinking of insect eyes.

"This isn't restricted in any way," Bonnie mumbled. "I can get anywhere. Response time is amazing as well. I'd love to have this at home if we could keep it connected, if we could even move it."

Marshall walked back over to the tub. Where did he know it from?

The tub itself was a lightweight plastic with high walls angled outwards on three sides, and a shorter wall where the vid camera looked in. Inside though, it was dressed like a command center. There was a throne, and deep blue velvet hangings covered the plastic walls. The items inside were hollow shells instead of actual command center equipment, but it looked convincing. It looked official, agency.

That's when he saw the pile of clothes in a corner of the tub room. He climbed in and picked them up.

"Bonnie? I think I know what all this is."

Bonnie didn't seem to hear him. She kept tapping at screens. "This has access to agency data," she said. "Looks like a flood apocalypse is coming, pretty quick. The polar ice caps are melting, fast. There's no reason listed. Most of the planet will be flooded in a matter of hours. Wonder why they haven't done anything yet? Weird to see the data before they act on it."

"You'll want to see this," he said, holding the clothes up, "even if a flood is coming."

She looked upward. "There hasn't been a broadcast yet, right? We would still have seen it." She turned back to the terminal setup. "I can't find any active alerts on here. Maybe they're getting ready for one. They've got to . . . given the planet is about to submerge."

"Bonnie."

She finally looked. Marshall held a long maroon dress coat and maroon slacks. Cording, the same color as the fabric, spider-webbed all over both. A shirt in his hand appeared to be woven from threads of silver. There was also a long gray wig and some artificial gray facial hair. He held the items away from himself, as if they were diseased, or covered in vomit.

Bonnie gasped. "Is that—"

"—Yeah." The one word seemed sufficient.

He'd realized why the room looked so familiar yet was so hard to place exactly. It was one he'd seen countless times, but hadn't ever been in. He'd never seen it with his actual eyes, always instead through a vid camera lens. That was harder to recognize, actually being there rather than seeing it in a broadcast.

It was weird, being there instead of perceiving it as it was designed to come across. A set. Props. Shells only appearing to have substance. Magisterial looking, but actually configured in a plastic tub.

It was the room where Malcolm filmed broadcast. The clothes? Malcolm's.

"Is this . . ." Bonnie breathed.

Well perhaps clothes wasn't accurate. The term described clothes, pants, and a shirt well enough, but the wig? The fake facial hair? All of it taken together as it was? Perhaps Malcolm's costume was a better phrase. Malcolm appeared to be as much presentation as the command room itself.

Bonnie looked at the costume, and then at the set. She scanned the vid equipment, and then the terminal setup. She paused in thought, continuing to look back and forth at everything, considering something. Pondering.

Marshall kept looking at the costume held away from his body. It revolted him though he wasn't sure why. Something about the entire scene bothered him, disturbed him on a preconscious level, but he struggled. He didn't feel it should have disturbed him. Whatever this suggested, nothing should have been different. There was simply something even more pointless about it all.

Still, it bothered him. The fact he was bothered, bothered him. Bonnie didn't seem phased. She was focused on something else. Marshall sucked it all down and forced the feelings onto the costume itself. That was easier to deal with and process—a kind of anti-talisman. Marshall didn't want emotional complexity or that many gray areas. He wanted things clean, comprehensible.

"Can you fit into it?" Bonnie asked.

"What?" The idea horrified him. "Why would I want to?"

"Just do it, try it on."

Marshall wanted to refuse, but he'd have to tell her why. Bonnie wouldn't have merely accepted any excuse. He would have had to figure out the reason, which he wanted to do even less than he wanted to wear the costume.

He shucked his clothes and put the disgusting thing on.

The silver shirt was designed for a smaller man, but it had a surprising amount of give to it. The result was tight, but he could get it on. The pants and coat weren't a problem either. They almost seemed constructed to fit a range of builds and heights, disguising the shorter and smaller, but with give for the bigger and taller. The legs were a bit high on his calves, but not noticeably so.

"Keep going," Bonnie instructed, pleasant but stern.

The wig was more of a challenge. He had hair already and the wig didn't seem fitted for that. Perhaps there was a skullcap around somewhere, though he hadn't found it. He managed to make it work eventually. It wouldn't have stayed in place if he ran around, but it was on. The facial hair adhered to his face though he hadn't felt any adhesive. That part was easier, at least from a practical standpoint.

"Now let me look at you."

Marshall stood straight, decked out as he was. He looked toward her, but not straight at her, looking beyond instead. Looking her in the eyes it didn't seem right. There was a different feeling to being in the costume.

"Dead ringer," she whispered. "You look just like him." She stared.

"Anybody would," Marshall grumped. "Maybe even you. Want to try it next?"

Marshall worried it was some fetish thing, wanting him to dress up like Malcolm. He didn't like that.

But, he didn't suppose he could fault Bonnie if it were the case. It was weird, but Malcolm was the most known face on the planet. Or, his image was at least. The dress up showed it wasn't so much the actual face. Still, Malcolm was the man in control. He held destinies. Should Marshall look down on Bonnie if she responded in some small way, if she wasn't completely free of the reactions most people had? He reflected even he had an emotional response to the get up.

Would he want to see Bonnie dressed up in it? He hoped he wouldn't.

"No time," she snapped. The awed look in her eyes was mercifully gone. "This isn't a game."

Marshall blinked. The facial hair itched. "Then what the hell am I doing?"

"You're going to be Malcolm," she responded. "No playing. You're going to be him."

She pointed at the vid equipment. "I think I've got the equipment figured out. If I'm right, I can vid you making a broadcast and actually send it out. Then I can jam the carrier media with a blank signal so the agency can't do a correction."

"Seems like a bit of a setback to save people," he mentioned.

Bonnie smiled wryly. "Who said it was going to be a helpful broadcast? You can say whatever you want. If the jamming works, you'll be the final word. That word will be law."

For a moment, Marshall felt a rush. He was glad when the feeling receded. He didn't want to like being Malcolm. It would have been as wrong as everything else. Maybe more so.

"I've got nothing to say," Marshall protested, "unless you want me to tell them what crap I think apocalypses are. I could, but I'm not sure even Malcolm saying it would help."

"No worries, Lunk." She smiled. "I didn't actually mean you could say what you want." She paused. "You could . . . but I had other ideas."

Marshall, or Malcolm he supposed for the moment, nodded. Somehow, that was better.

Bonnie positioned him on the set. She fiddled with the vid equipment, cursing occasionally. Then she tapped on some of the terminal set up screens and went back to fiddling with the vid equipment.

"You're sure you've got this figured out?"

"Shut up," she said. "I'll get it."

Marshall stood and waited where she'd placed him. At first, he tried to look impressive. Then he relaxed. He could be Malcolm when she was ready, no sense wasting the effort beforehand. It did seem to be an effort. He figured she probably should have placed him last.

Finally, she was satisfied with whatever it was she'd done with all the gear. She found the cue board and traced a few things on it to verify it worked. Then she tapped it to clear again.

She turned to face him.

"All right, we've got one shot at this," she told him, "presuming it works at all. I'm going to write on this thing and you'll read it. Got it? Don't act like you're reading. It's got to look like it comes from you."

"Got it," he responded.

"Don't look at anything going on around you. Not at me, the equipment, anything. Only look in the vid camera. We don't know what this stuff looks like when it's going so it might surprise you, but ignore it. And, whatever you do, don't check yourself out in the sky. That'd blow the illusion for sure."

"I said I've got it," he protested.

"Fine," she said. She tapped a few more screens. Then she held up the cue board and he went back to trying to look imposing. "Remember . . . be Malcolm," she said, flipping a switch and pointing to him.

The spotlight thing began to hum and glow. A light beam shot out from it, upward. An indicator light blinked on the vid equipment. They were live. Bonnie wrote on the cue board.

"Citizens." he read. He didn't know why he read that part. He knew it came first and could have done it on his own, but he read it anyway. Maybe the real Malcolm did it for the exact same reasons, Marshall thought.

"Citizens." he repeated, snapping himself out of the thought. "You are all in tremendous danger. An eruption of solar flares has altered the magnetic field of the earth. Our rotation is slowing rapidly, and our gravitational field is decreasing as a result."

Marshall almost stopped himself. That didn't make any sense. Solar flares didn't alter earth's magnetic fields. Even if they did, the planet's rotation wasn't dependent on the magnetic field, and gravity further dependent thereon. It was the opposite. The gravitational pull of the sun caused earth's rotations and the magnetic field resulted therefrom. It was all mixed up and didn't work.

But, then he remembered not to question. The science didn't have to work. People only had to believe it did. The spiel sounded half plausible, if you didn't think it through. People probably wouldn't. They were told wildly improbably things all the time. The information wasn't exactly subject to peer review and rigorous analysis. There was a significant chance people would buy it.

Besides, he'd already said it. Even if it didn't hold water, it was too late to fix. He needed to keep reading and not get lost in the details. Yet again, he needed to trust Bonnie . He'd come this far.

What was the worst that could happen?

The worst, he remembered, was a failure of the worst to happen. At least some of him still held back, so it was almost good either way.

"As gravity decreases, we will all become relatively lighter. Our connection to the planet's surface will weaken. There is a serious possibility we will begin floating off into space. If this happens," he paused, there was an instruction on the cue board to do so, "we will all die in the cold vacuum outside the atmosphere."

Bonnie flashed him an okay sign with her hand. Apparently, he was doing fine. He started to laugh, but restrained himself and kept reading.

"There is no time to avert the crisis itself, we need all citizens to act immediately to preserve themselves in the face of it. Find the lowest areas possible. Basements, gullies, dry wells, the lowest ground at hand. Go there. Strap yourselves to the heaviest objects you can possibly find. Lead weights, cement blocks, the more and heavier the better. Fix them as well as you can. They will do little good if you pull loose."

Low ground? Weights? Marshall wondered, but then he remembered a flood was coming. Then it all made sense. Horrible sense, but sense all the same. He tried to keep the expression on his face stoic, not let it show what was running through his mind.

Would people do it? Would they do it before they learned of the flood? Would they stay as instructed long enough? Marshall couldn't believe they would, but he knew it was likely they might. People did what Malcolm told them to, they always had. This might actually work, it really might.

"Only then do we stand a chance to avoid loss of our earth-bound status, and our lives. Only, and I repeat only, if the ground is low enough and sufficient extra mass is firmly enough attached do we stand a chance. Go. Go now. There is preciously little time."

Bonnie pressed one of the screens on the terminal set up. The indicator light on the vid equipment went dark and the spotlight thing powered down. Bonnie drew her hand sideways across her chest.

Marshall relaxed.

Bonnie held up the cue board one last time. It read: "And then the earth was wiped clean."

Interlude

I'm going to break in here and interrupt things again, because that's what I do. Besides . . . what is anyone going to do about it? I control the horizontal, I control the vertical.

Okay, no more obscure and antiquated references. Not everyone has the kind of archive access I do so nobody knows what I'm talking about, not that they would anyway . . . not that even I do.

I'm gibbering, probably as expected.

Still, I'm expected to be writing this. They probably won't read it. No one else probably will either. It's an exercise, a pointless activity. Supposedly, it's an important thing to do. Write down one's thoughts. At least this exercise doesn't require sweating, or special clothes. I have enough special clothes for my tastes. More than enough.

Had a bit of fun with them though. They asked how it was going and I told them it was done, thought recorded. Sat right down and got it done. Pretended to be surprised to learn they meant to do it more than once, a regular process. Faux shock.

That made them sputter a bit.

Really though, I don't see what they expect me to write. I'm just not sure I have any special thoughts. I have opinions, reactions, but thoughts? Contemplations? I sit down to write and find the tank empty. I don't know what they hoped I'd find.

As you can see, I'm repeating my start from last time, explaining what I'm doing. Explaining about the pointless thing they keep suggesting I do, for the sake of my mental conception of identity. Beyond that, I'll probably scribble for a while. Babble.

Would that satisfy them?

I suppose they won't know, since they won't read it. As long as I'm doing it, they'll be happy. It's not like they have any authority over me, but they do tend to whine endlessly if they don't get their way. That's irritating. So, let's make them happy. I'll satisfy the letter of their harangue, if not the spirit. I'm not trying to be difficult, but spirit is a little beyond me. That isn't my department.

Anyway. Got to make them think I'm doing something. No real thoughts to record beyond how useless this is, so what to do? Let's mix it up a bit this time. No more plagiarizing creation epics as a base and tap dancing on top. That's old hat.

I guess I'll make up a bunch of crap. Bear with me, I do apologize. This wasn't my idea.

Okay, make stuff up . . . let's start with two guys. Arnie and Oscar. A and O. Never mind who they are or what they look like. That isn't important or relevant right now.

Then again . . . none of this is.

Anyway, Arnie and Oscar had an elephant. They decided they wanted to measure it and figure out how long it was. It's important to know things like that about an elephant.

No, hold up a second. Nobody's going to believe Arnie and Oscar own an elephant. Those guys? Never. Who owns an elephant? There aren't even any around anymore. I doubt anyone knows what one is. They certainly won't believe those two clods owned one. No, let's revise. Arnie and Oscar didn't own an elephant.

They were hired to measure the elephant.

What can I say? I guess they should have tried harder in school. Studied more, been more ambitious. Heck of a thing to end up a measurer of elephants. Not exactly a dream job. Stay in school kids.

Anyway, they measured the elephant. For some reason, they didn't measure it at the same time, no one guy holding the elephant while the other measured. They did it separately. Maybe they weren't particularly organized. Then again, maybe they were trying for some kind of scientific accuracy. Measure twice and compare, or measure twice and average. Measure twice, cut once.

Wait . . . strike that last bit. This isn't that kind of story. Nobody cut the elephant. I wouldn't let them, even for pretend.

So they measured the elephant, which I reiterate was not theirs but, was in fact an elephant they were employed to measure. We need to be clear. They measured the elephant, and unfortunately they came up with different lengths, quite different. Arnie said it was twenty feet and Oscar got thirty.

Side note—please don't debate possible measurements on this. Don't look up information illustrating the average elephant was perhaps only ten feet long and insist there's no way they could have come up with twenty and thirty, respectively. Just don't do it.

First off, this is Arnie and Oscar we're talking about here. You know how screwy those two are. Second, none of my information gives me an exact figure to use for elephant length and I'm not going to take the time to track that sort of thing down.

Besides, this is a story. I can make an elephant any length I want to. Maybe it was an unusually long elephant, or an unusually small one, if it works out that way. In all actuality, I could probably make one whatever length I want now I think about it. Don't tempt me.

Anyway, Arnie measured twenty feet and Oscar measured thirty. Obviously, they were a bit miffed when they compared notes. Each had tried to do a good job measuring, and each insisted the other screwed the job up.

Of course, they went back to the elephant.

Arnie measured again, this time with Oscar watching. He did it from head to rump. He was meticulous, making sure the elephant didn't twist or move. Twenty feet, clearly.

Oscar immediately saw the problem. Surely anyone would have. Arnie hadn't included the elephant's tail, or its trunk. No wonder the elephant was only twenty feet for Arnie, he measured it wrong.

Demonstrating, Oscar got the elephant to come out at thirty feet. He lifted the trunk straight and measured. Then he measured the body, same as Arnie had. Finally, he went to measure the tail and added it all together. The answer was plain, the answer was thirty feet. Nothing could have been simpler.

Arnie protested. Anyone would have.

He insisted Oscar was the one going about things improperly. The trunk? The tail? Those weren't included in the length of an elephant. They were mere appendages, like legs. Only the main body and head should have counted.

Oscar disagreed.

Were the trunk and tail not parts of the elephant? Did they perhaps belong to another creature? No, the trunk and tail both needed to be included or the whole task was pointless. You couldn't go chopping off parts of an elephant willy-nilly.

Don't worry . . . that isn't where this is going. I promised you I wasn't going to let those jerks hurt the elephant, and I meant it.

Now, Arnie didn't disagree the trunk and tail were part of the elephant. He wasn't unreasonable. However, he adamantly maintained they should not be included in a measure of length. After all, they drooped. As such, they were associated more with height than length.

"Except when the elephant sticks them out straight," Oscar pointed out. If the elephant extends them, then they were length and not height. Thus, they should be measured.

Arnie saw a problem with this. An elephant should have a single length. That length should be a fixed number. Who had ever heard of a variable length elephant? Similarly, who'd ever heard of one with multiple possible lengths? The idea was ridiculous.

The trunk could be extended or allowed to droop. The tail was similarly flexible. Neither were either extended or drooped all of the time, unless possibly for an elephant with some kind of medical condition. Since the trunk and/or tail were only part of the length part of the time, either or both of them, neither should be counted. It was the only way a stable measure of length could be maintained.

Oscar saw Arnie's point, but he had issues of his own. He pointed out if they measured the elephant Arnie's way and the elephant then stuck out its tail or trunk, the elephant would then be longer than itself. That wouldn't work. What if someone needed the measurement to build a container for the elephant? The container could end up being too small.

Arnie asked why anyone would want to put the elephant in a container. Oscar told him not to split hairs.

Oscar did have a compromise to suggest. Why didn't they measure either the tail or the trunk but not both? Surely that was the elephant's most average state. Sometimes it drooped both the tail and the trunk and was only twenty feet. Other times it extended both and was thirty feet. Still other times it extended only one or the other and was thus twenty-five feet. Therefore, Arnie and Oscar should report twenty-five feet.

Breaking in to my own story again, please ignore the fact the elephant's tail and trunk were exactly the same length. I simply don't have that kind of data about elephants. Please assume they were on this one, or that Arnie and Oscar were total idiots. After all, they were.

Regardless, Arnie wasn't comfortable with this idea either. He felt the length of an elephant should be a precise thing. An average length simply wasn't precise enough.

The two weren't sure what to do. Each could see the other's point, but they could see their own more strongly. They wanted to do the job properly and weren't sure what measurement they should turn in, not wanting to mess up their first time on the job. Their employer had not provided instructions regarding this scenario, no exact definition as to what constituted the length of an elephant.

They were at an elephant impasse.

And honestly, so am I. I can't think of a way to resolve this for them. I've gotten things this far and can't think how to wrap it up. That's what comes from setting down one's thoughts. Sometimes they don't go anywhere. Besides, I'm not interested in solving their problem.

Let's scrap the whole thing.

Starting over, Oscar managed an apartment building. It was one of those ordinary multistory jobs. Had a basement too, and an elevator. Though not fancy, it was a decent enough place.

Now, decent enough didn't mean the place was perfect. Oscar did a good job, but there were plenty of tasks he hadn't gotten around to. Improvements needed to be made. Facilities needed to be maintained and hadn't been. Oscar simply couldn't be everywhere at once. The condition of the building hadn't gotten too bad, but he did need to get moving. Oscar was on the job, but some things simply hadn't been acted on as of yet.

For one thing, the walls of the ground floor were getting a bit faded. Let's say walls tended to stand long enough to fade in this time period. I know that sounds weird to anyone these days, but trust me—the walls were faded. It wasn't a dramatic failure on Oscar's part, merely something that got away from him. He needed to have them recolored.

Of course, as I mentioned, Oscar didn't have time. That's why the walls were faded in the first place. Also, he didn't have a pigment sprayer or any experience using one.

Oscar needed help.

It was fine thought. Arnie had both experience using a pigment sprayer and a pigment sprayer itself. He should have, given this was his job in this particular story. I know

I had them measuring elephants in the last one, but Oscar manages apartments and Arnie colors walls in this one. Call it a promotion, if you must.

Anyway, Oscar called Arnie on his communication unit. Hired him for the job. Arnie was thrilled, raring to go. Business had been slow lately and Arnie needed the work. He said he'd come over and do the job right away.

Now, that was fine with Oscar, but he was particularly busy right then. He didn't have time to show Arnie around the building. Still, it was no matter. Neither of them thought it was complicated. Oscar would give directions and Arnie would handle it on his own. Arnie was an experienced wall colorist.

So, Oscar gave Arnie the details. Building grid identifier, passcode, the works. Told him he wanted the same color as it already was, only fresh pigment. Just didn't want it faded.

They hung up and Arnie got his pigment sprayer. Rushed right over. Got in the building, went to the first floor, and got started.

He did a good job too, meticulous. The pigment was perfectly uniform and didn't have any blemishes. Not a speck on anything else that wasn't a wall. Not furniture, ceiling, or floor, utility plates, climate controls, nothing. Arnie was a professional. He was quick too. Done in about half the time other colorists might have taken. The color was perfectly matched, the same, but years brighter. Like new. It looked great. Unfortunately, he was on the wrong floor.

The fact was discovered when Oscar heard noise and came down to the basement. He found Arnie down there, amidst all the freshly colored walls, admiring his handiwork. He was done; he packed away and cleaned his color sprayer.

Mind you, Oscar passed through the ground floor to get there, obviously, since that's how one gets to a basement. Arnie expected admiration and to be paid. Instead, Oscar asked him why he did the basement and when he intended to do the first floor.

A difference of opinion commenced.

Oscar insisted they were in the basement and the ground floor was the first floor, the one he wanted colored. Arnie countered the basement was the very first floor of the building, and he colored as instructed. Thus, he should be paid.

There was a small bit of noise at that point.

Though the basement could perhaps have used a coloring, it was primarily a storage area. Tenants didn't go there much, certainly not as much as the lobby on the ground floor. That was what Oscar needed colored, what he was willing to pay for. As it stood, Oscar was in the exact same spot as before. He still had a faded lobby. As manager, he needed to make sure that was taken care of. The basement was irrelevant to Oscar.

But, Arnie had colored the walls of an entire floor. He was told to color the first floor of a building, and he did. He maintained he should be paid. It wasn't his fault Oscar referenced something as the first floor when it wasn't the bottom floor of the building.

Oscar disagreed. Ground floors were always referred to as the first floor. It was a convention and a universal one. Arnie should have known. What floor did he come in on? He didn't enter into the basement. Oscar could be sure, as the basement didn't have an outside entrance.

Arnie retorted if the convention was so universal, why wasn't Oscar's ground floor labeled first? It wasn't. It was labeled lobby on both the signs and in the elevator. Anyway, what was the basement? A different building? One all its own though it was connected? A negative floor?

But, Oscar seized on the elevator reference. Though the ground floor was listed in the elevator as lobby and the basement as basement, hadn't Arnie seen the other floors were two through ten? Shouldn't that have indicated to him ground was first?

In fact—oh, screw it. I don't feel much like finishing this one either. We all know Oscar's going to refuse payment and Arnie's going to file a lawsuit. What fun is left in this one?

I'm going to try again.

Okay, let's not have Oscar and Arnie have jobs. They're unemployed. They're not idle though, not those two guys. They're amateur historians.

Yes, people were once concerned with history. Don't make me explain.

Anyway, Arnie and Oscar decided they were going to write the history of their city. They got pens and a huge stack of paper. They researched. Then they sat and wrote and wrote and wrote.

Yes, people used to write on paper. Some still do, even if it isn't common. Just accept it.

Arnie and Oscar wrote for months. They wrote sitting at opposite sides of a table in a house they shared. They covered immense stacks of paper with their scrawling. They covered everything, in one way or another, from the formal incorporation of their city all the way up to their present day. It was all there, written on paper.

When they were done, they sat back in their chairs to take a breath and gaze at the pile of pages. There were quite a lot. Arnie and Oscar were amazed when they looked at it, and proud of themselves. Rightfully so, it was quite an achievement.

But, then it hit them, both at the same time. It wasn't complete. They tried to put in everything, but events got left out. That wasn't any good. Either it was merely a particular perspective on the city's history, which wasn't what they'd been trying to do, or it was comprehensive, which it wasn't. As thorough as they had been, they'd missed.

Did the city only begin at legal formation? Wasn't it a larger process? The city had been incorporated because a large enough group of people lived there that a city needed to be formed. It was the next logical step, and Arnie and Oscar couldn't begin partway up the staircase. They needed to begin at the bottom.

So, they went back to work. Again on opposite sides of the table. Reworking, writing, more writing. The page pile grew twice as tall as it had been before. Perhaps more. They went all the way back to the city's first settlers.

Also, time was still going forward as they worked. They couldn't stop where they had previously, what had once been the present, and call it done. No, if they wanted their history to be comprehensive, they had to keep going, take it up to their present.

Finally, Arnie and Oscar were done again. They sat back once more in their chairs and sighed with relief. It felt good, but it had been a great deal of hard work. Regardless, it was finished. Monumental as such a thing was, they had a comprehensive history of their city.

Except . . . they didn't.

They realized this in the midst of their celebration. What about the indigenous people who lived there before the first settlers of what eventually came to be the city arrived? They hadn't formed the city themselves, that was the settlers, and they'd lived a different way of life entirely, but hadn't they had an impact on the city? Didn't they have a hand in shaping it? Weren't they eventually, or their descendants, absorbed into the city?

The history wasn't complete until it went back and dealt with them as well. Moreover, it needed to cover what the indigenous people had done before they had come there and the same for the settlers. Arnie and Oscar had to go all the way back or the history would still only be partial.

They had to get writing again. Of course, the ending had to be brought forward more as more continued to happen.

Evolution before man came on the scene? The geological history of earth before life appeared? The formation of the planets and stars? The past became more remote and the future got later.

Arnie and Oscar were going to need more paper.

Hmmm, I looked back on this one, speaking of someone looking at something they had written. I think this one is actually worse than the other two. It's boring even to me.

Dump away.

Arnie and Oscar walked into a bar. . . .

Part III: Lenny Bruce is not Afraid

"I am filled with fear and tormented with terrible visions of pain. Everywhere people are hurting one another, the planet is rampant with injustices, whole societies plunder groups of their own people, mothers imprison sons, children perish while brothers war. O, woe."

WHAT IS THE MATTER WITH THAT, IF IT IS WHAT YOU WANT TO DO?

"But nobody wants it. Everybody hates it."

OH. WELL, THEN STOP.

At which moment She turned herself into an aspirin commercial and left The Polyfather stranded alone with his species."

—A SERMON ON ETHICS AND LOVE,"
Principia Discordia

"Of course, I'm crazy, but that doesn't mean I'm wrong. I'm mad but not ill"

-"Werewolf Bridge," Robert Anton Wilson

Chapter One

Marshall swallowed. He didn't know the next part of the plan, he'd not wanted to ask. Maybe it hadn't been decided yet. Perhaps Bonnie concentrated on the broadcast part, stayed in the moment since it all needed to be figured out so quickly, and hadn't yet thought of the question on Marshall's mind.

The big question.

Bonnie was back at the terminal setup. She watched the screens and tapped at them. For the most part, however, she watched the sky above through the aperture.

"Won't be long now," she mumbled though whether to him or in general he couldn't be sure. "Either it worked or it didn't. Nothing to do but wait."

Was that an answer to the unspoken question? Marshal wondered. It was an indirect one if so. Or, had it not occurred to her if there was a question and she was simply focused? Marshall wasn't sure whether or not he should voice it. Not asking might not change the answer, but asking would definitely change the character of the moments in between.

Were they going to high ground or not? They'd tried to trick the world into drowning, were they going to save themselves to see if it worked? Or, were they going to voluntarily submit themselves to the fate they'd wished upon the planet?

They'd accepted and understood to truly end things, to make it all stop; they unfortunately had to end as well. They were people and as long as any member of humanity existed, in even the tiniest number such as two, events could still be viewed as apocalypses. Only when no more intelligent beings existed to define an event as such instead of merely what happened.

At least, they'd verbally accepted this. They'd agreed on it.

Should they save themselves, or try, and wait to be sure they were the only remaining problem? If so, they'd have to finish things afterward if they truly were serious. If they weren't hypocrites.

After all, it might not have worked. If they did nothing to preserve their lives then they might be the only ones to go. They'd sacrifice themselves for nothing. The problem would go on though they would have the blessing of being unaware.

Did it matter? Was it any less suicide to simply stay where they were as opposed to doing something, making sure, and then joining humanity's fate later?

Marshall wavered. There was and there wasn't. It was easier not to have to actively seek death, but it was more cowardly, and seemingly less committed. They would lose the chance to try again if needed. He wished he had more time to decide.

Bonnie didn't appear to be suffering from any dilemmas. If she had any of those thoughts then she either didn't show it or they didn't affect her in the same way. Marshall was troubled. She didn't appear to be. She was focused.

There were dilemmas on top of dilemmas. Should they flee or not was one, but should he ask about fleeing or not was another. The two were intertwined, but separate. He had as much trouble fixing his course on one as the other.

He could stay silent and either decide for them or assume she already had, since Bonnie hadn't moved. It was resolute in one way, and not in another. Or, he could speak up and force the issue—remind her they needed to run if they were going to, or learn they weren't. Also both resolute and not. He went back and forth, and he despised himself for it.

Hold his peace and torment himself with wondering, or speak and risk tormenting himself with knowledge of what was coming?

Of course, he knew what was coming if he didn't ask. They were below ground with a giant opening above their heads. It wasn't in the top of a mountain. There was only one thing that could happen.

Finally, he decided he'd rather have the situation clear. Deciding to do what they were apparently doing, since they were still there, seemed better than dithering about. At least then he could collect himself and come to terms with it.

Wasn't that what all the others did in response to apocalypses? He wondered. Wasn't that what it all was? Was he giving this all a much bigger significance than it had to anyone but them personally?

He swallowed again. If so, then his fate was well deserved.

"Bonnie," he said in a monotone, emotionless, "should we get out of here?"

She looked at him steadily, tearing herself away from the enormous hole in the sky. Knowing. He decided she seemed sad.

"There's no time, Lunk . . . not according to the data coming in. It'd take too long to get out through the tunnels . . . and there's nothing to climb here in the silo. Besides," she paused, "where would we go?"

"Right."

"Even with the holes already cut in the fences, how long would it take to get to hills? They're miles away. There's no time."

"Right," he said again.

"Anyway," she continued, pointing up at the sky, "here's the only place I can see if they get around the jamming and manage to send out a broadcast to fix the trick. If we leave now, I won't be able to see, won't be able to adjust in response. I have to stay."

"Right." Why did he keep saying that? He felt like he should say something, but nothing seemed worthwhile. He had nothing.

"Hold tight, Lunk." She gave him a mournful smile. "We won't be waiting long."

She turned back to watching the sky though all that was up there was brightness, clouds, and blue. For the moment, no broadcast. Also for the moment, no water.

For the moment.

Marshall decided if it was going to happen, it'd happen while he was in his own clothes. No silver shirt, no maroon pants and coat, no wig and gray facial hair. He'd be himself. That was the way to go. He took off the hateful things and put his own, normal clothes back on.

Then he was ready. Or, he was as ready as he could be.

So this was to be his tomb, Marshall reflected. A missile silo. Was it any worse than any other place? The apartment? The factory? The snows? The other planet? It was impressive at least, spacious. It had a certain dignity.

Of course, the place didn't matter. In the end, it was all the same. There was no dignity in any of it, no way for it to happen that was actually better than any other. There was no method, no place, no final moment that changed the basic fact. The one, all-important fact was unchangeably identical regardless of anything else. Unalterable in the slightest degree, indifferent to anything outside of itself.

Anyway, it probably wasn't going to be his tomb, just the place of his death. After they drowned they'd doubtless be washed into the tunnels or out the top, out the mouth of the silo, most probably. They'd come to rest somewhere outside. Maybe their corpses would get caught on the fence, or perhaps somewhere further out if the floodwater was higher. There might not be a single place, floodwater and debris could easily tear them to pieces and scatter their remains.

There was no way to know though he supposed there was no reason to care about that part.

Marshall found himself unable to stop looking around, no matter how pointless he thought it was, though he despised how other people reacted in apocalypses. Likely, they were going to die this time. Unless the agency stopped the flood itself, it didn't seem probable any unforeseen rescue attempt would include the bottom of an abandoned missile silo. Even if they failed, this was probably it. He couldn't avoid taking a final glimpse at where it was going to happen, actual finality, for once.

Besides, he didn't have much else to do while waiting. Bonnie was occupied, importantly so. He was not. He couldn't even spend his last moments talking to her, not while she needed to be at the helm.

He was on his own.

Marshall touched the silo walls. They were cold and hard. He looked at the tub again, pretend life. He touched the vid equipment, instrument of his last interaction with the world. Well . . . sort of him. He toyed with the idea of sending an actual personal message as a send out. He touched the indicator light.

It went on.

A giant screen on the wall of the silo not visible before, apparently only detectable when powered, flashed on. Well, giant in relation to Bonnie and Marshall, tiny in relation to the silo itself. It was only about twenty feet tall and about the same across, starting out only ten feet or so above the floor. It towered above them, but the mouth of the silo further towered seeming miles above that. Marshall saw himself as Malcolm frozen on the screen.

Except . . . not himself. He wasn't being Malcolm anymore. Someone was though, and they weren't a still image on the screen. They were standing there, looking. Watching.

"Lunk. Stop touching," Bonnie exclaimed, seeing the screen. Then she saw Marshall had changed clothes and taken off the wig. She blinked. Then she looked slowly back to the screen.

Marshall backed away. Bonnie did as well. They stared, transfixed. Neither spoke.

The figure, Malcolm, didn't speak either. Maybe Malcolm couldn't see them. Nothing indicated he could, no sign of recognition there were viewers in front of the screen. Perhaps they'd activated some agency feed, dead air recording Malcolm before a broadcast. Marshall hoped, but then the figure's eyes went to each of theirs in turn. The figure cleared his throat.

"What do you people think you're doing?" Malcolm demanded.

Before Marshall or Bonnie could answer, an immense roar drowned out all sound. Marshall thought it was like being in the engine room of the space freighters, the impossibly loud clamor of machines. The light snapped, off, as if the aperture had closed.

Then, the waters poured in.

Marshall reflected it was like skydiving in reverse, or he guessed, since no one did that sort of thing anymore. Only, no chute. The slam of sudden impact, knocking the wind out of him. Buried alive, millions of gallons of water. No up, no down. Tumbling. Rushing. No way to see, cut off, spun by the uncomprehending water.

Marshall hadn't had a chance to take in a breath. The water slapped out any air he already had.

What good would it have done anyway? Under all that water? He'd never have been able to surface in time to breathe again. Even if his lungs had been full, it would have gone stale too fast. He would have had to take another breath while still under. His lungs would have filled with water.

It was all the same when Marshall's lungs filled on impact. Crushed, an involuntary wet breath. Choking. Vomiting. Reflexively gulping more water, desperately trying to breathe but no breath to be had. All the while thrown and spun, sucked and gushed. Currents and undercurrents, ever-present blackness. Tremendous pressure in his ears, in his head, in his chest. He couldn't separate them, though the idea of them was separate.

Bonnie. Where was Bonnie? Was she close? She could have been anywhere. Right by him, blasted all the way across the silo, shot into the tunnel. It made no difference though his gut reaction was to wonder. Even if she were right next to him, he could have done nothing for her.

He was powerless, as was she.

He expected to pass out, trying to choke and breathe, but he didn't. Time seemed to pass. He had no reference. Three seconds or a million.

Then he wasn't choking. He wasn't inhaling water and regurgitating it. There was no panic to take a breath. It was as if he was breathing already.

The sides of his neck and ribs burned.

He did not pass out. He did not die.

His body drifted where the water wanted to take it. After a while, the pull wasn't as turbulent. He tried a few strokes. He could think a little better, so he let his body go and figured out which direction it floated. Then he swam that way.

The water grew lighter, or it seemed so. It was still filled, clogged with mud. But the water seemed brighter, like he could almost see.

Was he still in the silo? Had he swum, or been blown, out?

Marshall surfaced. Air.

Water was everywhere. Brown and rolling, yet remarkably flat. Water. He could see no land at the horizons. Sky to sky water, nothing else. Blue and white and brown. A simple color palette. Well, there was also the sun.

He saw the tub room, somehow floating. He also saw Bonnie a ways off, struggling to swim. He paddled furiously over and grabbed her from behind. Pulling her over to the tub room, he somehow managed to toss her in. Then he marveled he was able to pull himself over the short side lip as well. It seemed impossible he pulled it off, but he did.

"Gills," Bonnie choked out. "Fucking gills. Nobody's going to be dead. No wonder they hadn't done anything."

Marshall noticed beads of blood bubble along lines on Bonnie's neck. He felt his own and found the same, his ribs too. Gills: unnoticeable, but there to tear open when needed. They had been obscured by a thin layer of skin. They were already congealing closed.

"When did they do that?" Marshall wondered.

"Probably ages ago," Bonnie spat. "There was one ancient apocalypse prophecy that was supposed to include a world flood and people evolving to a new form. Something about a calendar. The Apocalypse Amelioration Agency probably engineered these into us in case it ever happened."

"Doesn't matter," Marshall responded. "Still means it didn't work."

Bonnie nodded.

"So . . . what do we do?"

Bonnie looked around the tub, and then at the floodwaters spread out unendingly over the land. "I guess we wait, Lunk. Just sit and wait."

Chapter Two

Marshall and Bonnie lay back on the floor of the tub room and looked at the sky. There seemed to be little point in looking around for a while, it was all brown water. They couldn't steer the makeshift craft anyway. At the moment, they could drift.

A broadcast filled the sky, but they didn't worry about it too much. At least they could be sure a broadcast couldn't see them.

"Citizens." Malcolm boomed. "Melting ice caps have flooded earth. Due to a technical failure related to the flood, an old message about a sun flare problem was transmitted instead of the relevant warning. Luckily, the Apocalypse Amelioration Agency had already prepared you for flood. You are all safe, though wet."

Technical failure? Marshall wondered if there was any chance the agency actually thought that had happened. Had there ever been a sun flare apocalypse and they'd forgotten, essentially playing back an old recording from deep in their memories? No, it was a story so people didn't panic about someone trying to kill them. Aggression was swept under the rug. Still, would people not remember there hadn't been a solar flare incident? Would they believe it?

They would, Marshall realized. They really would.

No matter.

"Salvation is close at hand," Malcolm continued. "We have deployed state of the art refrigeration ships to the poles and the ice caps are reforming at this moment. The original cause of the melt eludes us for the moment, but we are close to solving the mystery and will soon correct that problem as well. As the ice caps begin to refreeze, the water level will rapidly fall. You may then return to your homes and begin whatever cleanup is required. Assistance will be available."

Obviously, Marshall thought, this didn't necessarily apply to everyone. Could they return home? And why not?

"The water will leave quickly," Malcolm concluded, "so take care. Be watchful and this will all soon be over."

Malcolm nodded and the sky was again blue. Marshall and Bonnie looked up at it for a while after the image was gone, primarily because there wasn't much else to look at. The movement of clouds beat out the expanse of water for visual interest. They could look at each other, but only for so long at a stretch, particularly without feeling awkward.

The tub drifted.

After a while, the water began to go down. At first, they weren't able to tell for sure, though they swore it felt that way. Motion. Later, they began to see the tops of things, hills and such. Then more appeared.

As points of reference again became available, they could tell the tub was drifting at a pretty good speed. Most of the time, though it didn't appear so, drifting might not have been the correct word. Speeding. They weren't sure how far they'd travelled from the silo. It might not have been much, but then again it could have been a great deal. Marshall and Bonnie had no real way of knowing for sure.

There was little to do but wait, nowhere to go until the water receded. They could have been discussing their plan of action— what to do next. They didn't. Marshall didn't broach the subject. The tub's motion made it more pleasant to sit and relax for a while.

Bonnie and Marshall didn't often do that.

The water continued to fall. Soon the tub bumped against hilltops and whatnot as it sped along. They could make out more and more of their surroundings as more of it popped above the water level. Finally, the water receded far enough the tub ran aground.

There was still too much water to leave the tub, but it wouldn't be much longer. The speed of the water's retreat was impressive. At the very least, they could again make out where they were. The floodwaters had carried them back toward town. They were pretty near the outskirts of the city, in fact.

They waited a little while longer, for the ground to be safe to walk on. Debris and silt were everywhere, it looked like the earth had been in a giant plastic bubble and someone had shaken it, jumbling everything. It was a mess.

Finally, Bonnie and Marshall leaped down from the tub. Their feet squished a bit on impact, but the ground beneath was solid.

Hitting the ground, each headed immediately in a different direction. Marshall headed toward town. Bonnie, headed away. They both halted when they saw the other wasn't following.

"Where're you going?" Marshall asked.

"Where are you going?"

"Home," Marshall replied. "It didn't work. So what? We go home until we figure out something else."

Bonnie rolled her eyes. "Something else? What else? What's going to work? You know of another missile? It wouldn't do any good anyway. We'll turn out to have some new organ for surviving nuclear blasts we didn't know about. We've got nothing, Lunk. We're dry . . . so to speak."

Marshall leaned back against the wall of the tub. He sighed. "I don't know," he said. "So just throw it in?"

She shrugged. "I don't know what else."

"Go back. Wait. If something else comes up, try it. If it doesn't, keep waiting. Something has to work at some point. The Apocalypse Amelioration Agency is fallible. We've proved that much. Sooner or later, we'll get something past them, despite evidence to the contrary."

"You actually believe that?"

"I don't have a lot of other options."

Bonnie folded her arms over her chest, but didn't otherwise respond. She looked toward the direction in which she'd been heading, and then toward town. The one thing she didn't look at was Marshall.

"Neither do you," he continued.

"All right. You don't need to say it." She grimaced. "What makes you think we can go back? They never noticed the laxative, but they noticed this. Official story aside, he saw us."

Marshall thought for a moment. "True, but so what? He saw two people in a dark room. He never said our names. We don't know he has any idea who we are. We could be any two idiots. Do we assume he knows everything?"

"Maybe he does and maybe he doesn't. Do we take the chance? They could be waiting for us."

"They could," Marshall agreed, "but what if they're not? Going back is the only way to know. I'd kind of like to be sure."

"Some certainty is painful," she reminded.

"Well, even if they did get us, we don't know what they'd do. They could kill us, lock us up, politely ask us not to do it again, anything. There's no telling with the agency. Still, I'm not all that scared of them for some reason."

"I'm not either."

"Exactly." Marshall smiled. "Then we don't risk much by finding out."

"I guess," Bonnie mumbled.

Marshall thought she seemed more pissed than anything else. She was fed up and wanted to walk away from it all, wash her hands of it, and them. That was more likely than her fearing, particularly of any specific consequence. And, Marshall could understand. He empathized. But, did they have the luxury of throwing a fit? He supposed they could if they wanted, but only if they were willing to be self-indulgent. Supposedly they wanted to accomplish something.

"Besides," he argued, "where would we go? On the run? The lamb? Can people even do that anymore? The agency is in every city, it's not like we know anyone who'd hide us, if anyone could. Absent some apocalypse where they were too busy to keep track of people, which happens from time to time, we'd be found anywhere. We could go into the wilderness, but neither of us knows how to live there. There's no guarantee we wouldn't be found there eventually, anyway.

"Point," she muttered.

"Unless. . . ." he trailed off.

"Unless," she said.

"And in that case," Marshall went on, "I definitely want to be sure they're after us and there's nothing else to try. Short of any risk they'd torture us, which I've never heard of, we'd simply make certain the worst they could do."

Bonnie squished her feet around in the mud.

"I mean, I can't keep going with the way things are either, but that's the end, the final step. I'm in no hurry to get there any earlier than we have to, certainly not if there's more we could possibly do. It'd make it all that much more pointless and stupid."

"Point again," she reluctantly agreed.

It seemed to Marshall they agreed on everything then. No matter how much Bonnie didn't like it, there was no argument. That was fine. Marshall didn't care for it either. He didn't have to. But, it was the best of a shitty situation. Unless there was more, they should get going.

However, Marshall noted they still hadn't moved.

"So . . . home then?" He finally asked.

"Fine." she snapped and started walking quickly. Marshall thought she was about to argue more and was left behind. He hurried to catch up.

Bonnie showed no signs of slowing. She marched intently. Apparently, if she had to go back, she'd go back furious. Chip on her shoulder. Marshall followed along.

Whether or not they had fears, whether or not they believed they were walking into a trap, whether or not they pretended not to care, they were silent as they walked. Everything had been said, but they were busy. They kept their eyes open, watching people once those appeared, watching for anyone watching for them.

If anyone was, no one made a sign. Everyone went about as normal, or as normal as cleaning up after a flood apocalypse could be. Shoveling away silt, throwing away water damaged goods. Normal. No one looked at them, they didn't have time.

There was a tiny, tiny chance people had been told to look for them, but to hide it well. Marshall thought of that, but discounted it quickly. Most of those people didn't strike him as very good actors, restraining emotion.

Still, Bonnie and Marshall were wary. They kept carefully aware of where they were.

In fact, they walked the whole way back instead of taking the transport pod. Until certainty was achieved, it would be too easy to be trapped. Control of the pod was automated and under agency direction. Monitored. Routed. Already locked in, the agency wouldn't need to come and get them. Bonnie and Marshall would be sent to where ever the agency wanted them.

Marshall had seen that already.

No, they walked. That was safer. If they were going to be taken . . . they wouldn't simply deliver themselves.

As they neared the apartment, Bonnie spoke up. "You're sure? Nothing so far, but if we get closer and they are waiting, we might not get away. We can still turn back."

"Yeah," Marshall replied. "It's the only way to know."

They joined hands. Their speed slowed. They turned a corner and their building came into view. Their breath quickened. They stopped.

The building was surrounded.

The structure was encompassed by tight cordon of soldiers each standing about a foot apart. Individuals wandered both within and around the perimeter of the line. Other soldiers were stationed on nearby rooftops. All were in full battle armor, complete with full weaponry. Marshall may have been imagining it, but they looked ready to shoot.

"Shit."

"Well," Marshall weakly tried to joke, "what do you suppose the chances are they're here for some reason other than us?"

Then, one of the soldiers burst into flame.

Chapter Three

The soldier caught fire and Marshall looked to Bonnie. His first thought was she'd shot the guy with something, some flame weapon she'd scavenged somewhere and not shown him before. She wasn't holding anything though. In fact, she was looking right back at him. Apparently, she'd been thinking the reverse.

If not them, who?

The soldier, screaming, fell to the ground. He rolled quickly and the fire began to go out. He didn't look terribly hurt, but his screams didn't abate. Either he was in more pain than it appeared or he was pretty freaked out about it. Marshall guessed the latter.

The other soldiers milled about in confusion. The neat line broke, but the general rank maintained, the cordon kept for the most part. Some tried to help, some of the close soldiers, but there was little more they could do than pat at the flaming guy on the ground. Others pointed their shock rifles off at various places. Down the street, rooftops, wherever they guessed the attack had come from. None of them seemed sure. Still others were merely looking around, unable to decide what to do.

Where had the attack come from? Marshall couldn't figure it out. The only people around the building with weapons were soldiers, the rooftops as well. The only other people were citizens, and they weren't carrying anything capable of flame attack. There was no visible gunman.

There hadn't been any trail of fire for him to trace back to a source, no path of transmission. It came out of nowhere, directly on the soldier. One moment the guy wasn't burning and the next he was.

Well, Marshall wasn't sure if the soldier was a guy. There were both male and female soldiers, but they were all guys because the armor was shaped that way. Actual gender, or personal identity, was obscured. Marshall was shocked he was thinking about gender right then.

Bonnie looked around for the gunman as well, wildly. Marshall surmised she couldn't spot him either, nor had any more idea where to look. Her gaze certainly didn't focus anywhere.

Was there an attacker? If so, who? Who could be trying to help them?

Would anyone try to help them? What purpose would it serve? Create a distraction so Marshall and Bonnie could slip inside? They'd be trapped if they went for it. Take the soldiers out one at a time? A temporary solution at best, the agency would send more. There were always more soldiers.

It didn't make sense.

Maybe the flames were merely for the sake of havoc. That was at least a possibility. Someone was just creating it, regardless of whether or not it helped Bonnie and Marshall. Havoc didn't have to make sense. It didn't have to be related.

Perhaps the soldiers weren't there for them. Maybe it was a coincidence Marshall and Bonnie's building was surrounded. Someone might have gone rogue with a fire weapon and the soldiers were there to take care of it. That would definitely be something the agency would want to get on top of.

Then another soldier went up, a sudden burst of flames.

It didn't come from anywhere, Marshall didn't understand. Something as basic as a flamethrower would have had a fire jet travelling from some point of origin. An incendiary bomb would have been fired from somewhere they could see. Most energy weapons that heated a target had some sort of visible arc, a distortion of air in between. The fire had to be coming from somewhere. Fires didn't merely start out of nothing.

Marshall wondered if he'd missed it the first time, not been paying enough attention, and the fire spread from the first soldier to the second. Maybe the second hadn't been attacked, but was an accidental result of the first's flame. That was reasonable. As much attention as Marshall had been paying to the soldiers, he hadn't been thinking the soldiers could be attacked. He hadn't been watching for something like that.

Except, the two burning men hadn't been close to each other. The first was almost completely out by the time the second went up. There were even soldiers in between the two, who were fine. Unless the fire had jumped, that wasn't it either.

The soldiers panicked. The cordon broke up. Soldiers ran around. A few took shots though not at anything specific Marshall could identify. They certainly didn't hit anybody. Sides of buildings, the sky, signs, pretty much anything but a person.

Then a soldier on one of the roofs caught fire. Then another burst into flames on a completely different roof. More followed in what had been the cordon, soldiers on fire all over the place.

Everywhere, soldiers burst into flames, then stopped, dropped, and rolled. Some found water to throw on themselves, that seemed to work as well. No one seemed to be dying or getting severely injured. The fires were apparently not so fast or hot as to be immediately deadly, and they could be put out.

The fires cropped up everywhere among the soldiers. There wasn't any rhyme or reason to it, no way of predicting.

Then citizens started catching fire as well. All over the place, random people were burning. Marshall worried it would be deadlier for them, not having battle armor, but the effects appeared to be largely the same. People caught fire, people put themselves out. Still, that didn't stop the panic. Chaos reigned.

Marshall was fascinated. He couldn't stop staring at it all. It was strange, random. Bonnie hadn't said anything or made a move, so he imagined she was entranced as well. He didn't want to be. They should have taken advantage of the mess to run. Even thinking that though, fully aware, he couldn't look away. He couldn't make his muscles move.

Fire.

There truly didn't seem to be an attacker, Marshall reflected. No nut with a strange new weapon. He still didn't see anyone. Could someone stay hidden that long? Marshall didn't think so. It was too happenstance for human intention, too uncontrolled. For whatever reason, people were simply catching on fire. That was a new fact of life, something people had to get used to. Another annoyance, a potentially fatal one.

Marshall felt warm.

Time slowed down for Marshall. He felt warm, really warm. That was strange. The day wasn't exactly cold, but there had been a slight chill in the air. At the very least, the dampness from the flood brisked things up. Weird to be warm. Sure, people were catching fire all over the place, but none of them were nearby. Surely, even with that many people burning, not that much heat could be coming off them.

People were catching fire everywhere. Hmmm.

Hmmm. Marshall was feeling pretty warm.

He screamed and pulled Bonnie into a trench next to them. It was a dip between the street and the sidewalk, a depression formed when the street experienced subsidence issues and hadn't been fixed yet, but it was currently filled with undried floodwater. They splashed down, pulled by Marshall's momentum, and submerged.

Bonnie shot out again, spitting out water. "What the hell are you doing? Trying to kill us?"

"I felt warm," Marshall explained, having surfaced himself. He shook water out of his hair.

"So?"

"I was about to burn. Didn't you feel it?"

"No. I didn't feel anything," she exclaimed. "I was just starting to dry off. I . . . hold on. . . now I'm feeling hot."

Marshall grabbed her and dunked the two of them again. That time they were both ready for it and took a breath before going under. He held them there for a moment before surfacing again. The trench wasn't deep, but it sufficed.

"Better?"

"Yeah," she responded. "I'm definitely not hot now. I get what you meant thought. I was heating up all of a sudden. Is that what happens?"

Marshall shrugged. "Don't know, but I was warm for no reason and it was the only thing I thought of so I dunked us. It seemed reasonable."

"Well, we haven't actually caught fire yet," she noted. "Maybe you're right. I suppose better safe than afire, though I'm still pissed you didn't say something first.

Marshall smiled. "There may have been a little fun mixed in there. We need to do something though. I reacted, but it could keep happening. We can't stay here and keep dunking whenever we feel warm. Sooner or later, we'll need to leave this spot or sleep."

"Got to be something better than a three second solution."

The screaming around them continued. Soldiers and citizens ran around. One soldier who'd been on fire before burst aflame again.

"We need to get out of here," Bonnie commented. "Get away from so many people. At some point, they'll get whatever this is under control and start looking for us again."

"Agreed."

"We need a more private body of water. Somewhere we can wait this out," she muttered.

"The pond in the park?"

"That's disgusting." she retorted.

"Burning is pretty disgusting."

"Point," she conceded, "but how do we make it there? Merely roll when we burn? It's a long way."

Marshall took his turn conceding a point. He found a couple buckets in the flood debris. He handed one to Bonnie and they filled them from the trench. Then they marched off.

They kept away from clusters of people, more from the fear someone would need the water from their buckets than anything else. When Bonnie and Marshall started heating, they doused themselves. Whenever they saw water they could nab, they refilled the buckets.

Once or twice, they were caught warm with empty buckets, but rolling worked as a last resort. Still being wet helped reduce potential damage. The fact it only seemed to happen to one of them at a time helped as well, leaving the non-burning one available to put the other out. It wasn't the best way to live, but they got through.

Then they found water again and things were easier once more.

Flood then fire, Marshall found himself thinking as they went. Surprisingly, as much as they had to concentrate to avoid incineration, Marshall's thoughts wandered. It wasn't like they could effectively chat. Flood then fire, too much of one thing and then too much of the opposite. At least the apocalypses showed variety once in a while. Be careful what you wish for though.

Sooner or later, Marshall knew they'd have to come up with a longer-term plan. He should have been thinking about that instead of reflecting on apocalypses complementing each other in odd ways. His thoughts weren't easily guided though.

"Flambé," Bonnie said suddenly, apparently bored with merely trying to stay alive.

"Char broiled," Marshall responded, picking up the game.

"Blackened."

"Flame-grilled."

It was an odd game, Marshall decided, but oddly appealing. Different fire cooking techniques fired back and forth while they were under constant threat of incineration. They were weird people, Marshall concluded. As much as everyone else irritated him, Marshall had to admit he and Bonnie were weird.

The pond was close, the park in sight, when it began to rain. It hadn't even looked cloudy, at least not that they'd noticed. Then the skies opened up. A cloudburst.

"The agency," Bonnie concluded.

Marshall nodded.

They weren't surprised when Malcolm appeared. The rain didn't obscure his image. Nor did the clouds that had seemingly appeared from nowhere. They could see him plainly. When he spoke, they heard him clearly over the rain.

"Citizens. Do not be afraid, listen. The rains we brought will keep you from burning. It is safe to pause; you will not die during this broadcast."

Marshall noticed even Malcolm appeared wet. Something not within frame was casting a mist constantly on him, a light one. Apparently Malcolm was not immune to their problems though he didn't have to sit out in the rain. Then again, Marshall wondered if Malcolm was being misted to look as if he was afraid of catching fire. It was obviously intended to be noticed.

"Tragically," Malcolm said, frowning, "the Apocalypse Amelioration Agency is itself responsible for our current plight. The root cause is one of the refrigerant chemicals being used to refreeze the polar regions. Though it is inert and was believed not harmful to life, there has been an unexpected side effect."

Of course, Marshall thought. He bet Bonnie thought the same thing.

"The amounts utilized necessarily resulted in widespread exposure," Malcolm continued. "This should not have caused a problem. However, the human body mysteriously transforms the chemical. It takes in the inert compound, rapidly processes it, and excretes a highly flammable derivative through the skin. This derivative evaporates almost instantaneously upon contact with air, surrounding a subject with a flammable gaseous cloud. Any trigger, whether open flame, excessive heat, or even static electricity, can set it off. Bottom line? For the moment, we are all extremely unstable."

"How do we tell the difference?" Marshall whispered to Bonnie, both momentarily forgetting the seriousness of the situation and the fact there was no one around to overhear the joke. She laughed, loud.

"A solution is being developed. In any event, the poles will soon stabilize and the chemical will no longer be necessary. Even if no other remedy is found, the situation will abate once the chemical is no longer present. Until such time, however, or until another fix is found, we will continue to burn."

Malcolm signaled someone who couldn't be seen in the image. The amount of mist increased. Small rivulets dripped down the lapels of his coat.

"The rain we sent is sufficient for the moment, but we cannot maintain it forever. These are temporary measures to get you to safety. Even if we could, constant rain would bring back the floods."

Malcolm shook his head. Clearly, that wouldn't do.

"Every city, by design, is built near a bay on the sea. Go there. If you are not close to your respective bay, find one of the rivers leading to it. Or one of the canals leading to a river. Be careful of currents in the rivers, but the bays will keep you protected once reached. Remember, though uncomfortable to initiate, you can breathe underwater with your gills. The rains will aid you until you can get under, but do not delay. We must stop the rain soon."

Malcolm vanished. Marshall and Bonnie were left alone in the rain.

Marshall and Bonnie looked at each other. Pond or bay? They silently asked each other. The bay risked discovery, but they both realized the pond had no food.

"Risk it?" Marshall asked.

Bonnie smirked. "Why not? No one will be able to talk down there. That'll make looking for us pretty difficult for a while."

As they started walking toward the nearest river, Marshall imagined what the undersea settlement would be like. The lack of talking would be definite, and a plus. Living like that, he almost wondered if he could tolerate the others.

Chapter Four

Life in the sea required a few adjustments.

At least no one was looking for them there as far as they could tell. No one showed up or asked any questions. It gave Marshall and Bonnie a chance to relax and think while they figured out their next move. The situation was far from permanent, but that was kind of the idea.

The gills were only uncomfortable when they first came out. The body did not remember it could breathe that way. They choked, and vomited, with the sensation of drowning. Their skin tore open where the gills were, but once the body became accustomed, it was actually kind of nice. You didn't have to remember to breathe, or to drink. It just happened and you didn't notice.

One less daily complication to deal with.

Marshall found he could surface and come back without having to go through the changeover again, as long as he didn't stay out too long. The trick was to make sure the gill flaps didn't congeal shut. The blood was only from the initial tearing, but there was some kind of mucous in the flap that would seal shut if it dried. Making sure it didn't was the trick.

It took Marshall a few unpleasant episodes to learn, even with making sure not to stay out so long he caught fire. Still, with all the choking and vomiting, he learned pretty quick.

There also appeared to be a film over his eyes. He hadn't noticed it up on land, but it kept his eyes from getting irritated underneath. The film seemed to thicken some after he'd been under for a bit. His ears too. Something kept water out.

The breathing underwater got easier after he cut holes in the sides of his shirt. It only made sense, water needing to pass the rib gills and all, but it hadn't occurred to him initially. Or to anyone else either, from the looks of it. He swam with his shirt off one time, noticed the difference, and cut holes. Other people copied him. He was surprised the agency hadn't suggested it themselves.

They were the ones who made the gills.

Marshall still felt it was too much like living in fishbowl, like the setups people used to have. There wasn't an aerator or colored gravel, but the buildings had a similar feel. At least no one spread food flakes on the surface of the bay for people to come and eat. There was that, though Marshall supposed food was food in the end.

The buildings though, Marshall wasn't sure why they even built any in the bay. At first people only gathered together, but soon they began to build. Perhaps it was instinct.

Structures didn't serve the same functions in the bay as on land. There was no rain or snow underwater. No weather to keep out with a roof and such. That was probably good, because the sort of buildings people managed wouldn't have been able to do that anyway. The buildings were too tossed together.

It wasn't like people could make anything long lasting out of wood under water. Mortar wasn't an option, or sealants. People could make brief trips out for materials, but most didn't work well when wet. For the few that did, it was hard to get them placed right amidst the water currents. The floating didn't help either.

Construction was mainly from stacking rocks. There were plenty of rocks on the floor of the bay. Given they were underwater, they were actually able to move much bigger rocks than if they'd been on land. Marshall contemplated whether or not gravity manipulation could be similarly exploited when they were eventually back on land to increase industrial capacities.

Anyway, people stacked rocks. Sometimes the stacking was done well and structures were made that wouldn't immediately fall down, even without mortar or similar goop. Sometimes, however, it was not. Nobody usually ended up hurt when things did collapse, so that was okay. People got the hang of rock stacking eventually.

There was only so much to do underwater besides build, get food, and eat. People had to occupy time.

The structures looked like broken-down castles, being mostly heaped rocks. That didn't help much with the whole fishbowl feel.

Windows were made from holes in walls by stacking larger rocks over the gaps between two other rocks. Ceilings, when they were accomplished, were generally long bits of found things like driftwood placed atop rock walls with more rocks heaped over that. It would rot eventually, but people kept an eye out and maintained. The tops of walls were jagged. Very ruined castle.

The elements wouldn't have been kept out by such half-completed buildings on land, but there wasn't much to keep out. The big worry was water temperature, given most heating device technology didn't work submerged, but the bay was mild. Anyway, the agency announced plans to put an automated water-heating factory on shore to dump into the bay if the temperature worsened.

Marshall decided the main function of the buildings down there was privacy. That, and something to keep people contained so currents didn't snag anyone while they slept.

Privacy was something people relied on. As much as it went away during apocalypse copulation and/or rioting, people wanted privacy the moment none of that was going on. People were used to it. Rock piles didn't provide much protection, but they obscured the visual. Hanging out in a big group after a spontaneous combustion apocalypse was fine, but walls went up shortly thereafter.

Of course, it wasn't as if someone couldn't merely look through the cracks if he or she wanted to. As mentioned, construction was shoddy. Still, Marshall reflected the idea of privacy seemed more important than any actuality. Rocks provided that much and people seemed satisfied.

Again, at least someone wasn't sprinkling flakes on the water's surface.

At first, Marshall worried the Apocalypse Amelioration Agency might do exactly that. After all, where was food to come from? Though not all surface food made it down intact, some did. Foraging trips, performed under water protocols to prevent burning, got people supplies.

Surprisingly too, there were fish and other creatures in the bay, algae. These must have come back since the last time an apocalypse decimated them. Either that, or the agency had replenished them. Either way.

Fishing underwater took a bit of learning, but people got the hang of it. The electronic fishing apparatuses once used were pointless, even when waterproofed, but people remembered some of the older techniques. Barbed spears were easy. Water nets took more practice, but soon caught on. Both were made on shore and then brought down. People actually learned to do something for themselves for once.

The algae and other underwater plants were, of course, easier to catch. Those didn't run away, or attack. They just needed to be gathered from beds or whatnot, and underwater plants lasted a while after harvesting. People weren't fond of the tastes, but the mostly fish diet was well supplemented.

Critters brought around the idea of protection again. Rock piles wouldn't keep fish or such out, though since so many people collected in one spot, fish tended to avoid the immediate area. That kept people safe and un-irritated, though it did mean hunters had to roam a ways from the colony.

All in all, life wasn't bad. People seemed to stomach it okay. Marshall and Bonnie were even included among people in that regard.

Of course, the somewhat idyllic feel of the colony was spoiled for Marshall and Bonnie by the memory of what they still needed to do. Hanging out with the fishes to preserve their skins was all fine and good, but they knew they needed to get back to the task of ending the world. Hiding forever, even if possible, wasn't what they wanted. At least, it wasn't enough.

Besides, they knew they wouldn't be able to hide for much longer. Sooner or later, there'd be another apocalypse or the spontaneous combustion apocalypse would end and people would move back to land. Bonnie and Marshall would likely be found then, as the agency would probably search for them again.

There was the chance people would choose to permanently stay in the sea even when the combustion apocalypse was over. People would decide they liked it better down below.

It was nice down there.

Doubtless the agency would someday find a way to return things to normal under the water as well. Marshall understood this. Devices would be adapted, connections laid. Given enough time, hiding in the bay would be as difficult as on land.

Presuming anyone cared about them then.

Bonnie and Marshall rarely left the water, and didn't tend to join in the surface-side scavenging trips. Marshall tried not to think about it, and pretended it was so they wouldn't have to tell anyone who they were. On some level though, he recognized it was so they couldn't talk to each other either. If Bonnie and Marshall didn't talk, they didn't have to go back to figuring out what came next.

It was a bit like a seaside vacation.

Marshall and Bonnie had their own little rock pile. They had barbed spears, nets, and fish. Algae. They acted as if it was temporary, but each worried they were a little too willing for it to be more.

Until the time came when they no longer had a choice. They waited too long, the situation changed. Decisions were made for them.

Foraging parties discovered people no longer heated when out of water. It hadn't been noticed at first, not burning being less obvious than burning, but people eventually began to realize they'd gone whole trips without dousing themselves. The implications were clear, but caution remained. Perhaps chemical levels had only lowered so the effects were not as quick but still would occur with longer lengths of exposure.

No one immediately rushed to dry land.

Still, some wanted to test it out. They sat up on the beaches, close to the water line, with containers of water nearby. Others watched anxiously from the water's edge as the testers waited. The testers sat, slept while helpers watched over them with buckets, and then woke to sit more. After testers remained unburned after several days running, it was commonly decided the spontaneous combustion apocalypse was no more.

Land was safe again.

Marshall hated people calling it that, the spontaneous combustion apocalypse. He'd done it too, but that didn't make him despise it any less. If anything, it made him feel worse. The term simply wasn't accurate.

People didn't truly believe in spontaneous combustion anymore, though they remembered the phrase. It was antiquated, an out of date superstition. No one burst into flames without reason, people knew this. There was always a cause, always. And, though people were certain of the cause in the present case, and the term referred to no cause situations, they still used it. Marshall used it.

But, it was over anyway. People didn't burn anymore unless they set themselves on fire. There was little enough reason to keep using the term, and increasingly less reason for Marshall to get upset about it.

However, the water was draining out of the tub.

People began moving from the bay back to their homes. It started slowly, not everyone en masse, but it happened. Steadily, and in increasing numbers.

Bonnie and Marshall realized they needed to face the situation. They couldn't simply return to the apartment, obviously, but they couldn't stay where they were either. Even if no one was waiting at home anymore, it was too likely a location for someone to check at some future time. But, it would also be pretty noticeable if only two people chose to remain in the bay. They needed to act before that became the case.

They overheard a conversation on one of the few trips Bonnie and Marshall took above the waterline. They still hadn't gone on any foraging trips, or gone much further than the shoreline, but they started going up once in a while to hang around the beach where those still living underwater went to talk, trying to find out rumors of what was going on up on land.

As it happened, the flood apocalypse before the spontaneous combustion apocalypse had taken out homes in some areas. To assist, the Apocalypse Amelioration Agency built some quick block housing. It wasn't much, but it was a place for people to go.

Now, that alone wouldn't have been of use for Bonnie and Marshall, necessitating a walk straight into the agency. However, the flood had also taken out many agency databases. Apparently, the block housing assignment offices were also able to register people whose records had been lost. Marshall saw opportunity.

Bonnie was more hesitant. Even if false names were given to obtain new identities, surely biometrics would be recorded. Sooner or later, someone would cross check against existing records, and make sure someone hadn't done what Bonnie and Marshall intended to do.

However, reports also came back about the swamped working conditions at those offices. Many more homes had been destroyed, and identities lost, than it had first seemed. Either that, or more people than expected wanted to change homes and/or identities. In order to keep up, offices temporarily omitted biometric collection. The agency stated such would likely be collected later anyway in the ordinary course of affairs.

Bonnie and Marshall went for it.

Sure enough, no biometrics. Marshall and Bonnie received new names and a shared spot in block housing. Marshall picked Bo, something with as few letters as possible so he could recall it easier. Bonnie picked Shelly. She didn't explain why.

They were safe for the time being, and it was time to get back on track again.

They only trusted the block housing so far. Walls were thin. People might overhear if they planned there, and they could only speculate as to whether or not the agency had put in monitoring devices. Trust wasn't possible until they knew more.

They went back to the old park in order to talk. It was relatively undamaged by the flood though some of the trees had died, and it was still fairly unfrequented by people. It seemed risky to go back into old habits, but no one knew they used to go there. They knew of no recording devices in the area, and no one had been there to see them. Besides, they figured they had to take some chances if they were going to end the world. As a result, the park became a frequent visit.

Unfortunately they still hadn't had any ideas.

"Nothing, Lunk?" Bonnie asked one day as they sat on the shores of the park pond yet again.

"Hey," he shot back, "I came up with the ICBM. I told you I had one idea. I'm tapped out."

"Yeah," she grumbled, "that worked out so well anyway."

"Not my fault." He leaned back on some dead grass.

Most of the park grass had died, but it hadn't rotted. It was merely dried out and brown. Floods were not great for lawns and other such plants.

Then the earth began to rumble like someone grabbed the ground and gave it a good shake. Steam rose from the pond, which began to bubble. The island in the center swelled. Cracks appeared in the ground, smoke billowed out. Magma shot upward.

Bonnie and Marshall ran.

"A volcano," she screamed as they fled. "Are you fucking kidding me?"

Marshall didn't respond, choosing instead to concentrate on running. It didn't seem like she was expecting a real answer anyway.

The rumbling continued, coming from all around them. More ground swelled beneath their feet, and smoke was everywhere. There was more magma. Marshall realized, chagrined, it was another apocalypse—a volcanic apocalypse.

The sun went black. Everything was black. They couldn't see. Marshall and Bonnie linked hands, changing direction to hopefully avoid lava rivers when there was too much heat in front of them. There were explosions.

Marshall and Bonnie instinctively ran for the block housing, at first. Then they were simply running. Away. Anywhere. Away from the smoke, lava, and explosions. There wasn't anywhere to run to, but they weren't thinking that far ahead. It was only running.

"Citizens." Malcolm's voice boomed from above, though his image wasn't visible. Volcanic smoke was evidently one thing capable of obscuring a broadcast.

"Citizens," Malcolm repeated. "We are in the middle of an immense geologic event. Waste no time, head to the city centers. Ships are waiting to take everyone into orbit where we will all safely wait for this to pass. There is no time to organize, board the first ship you find. Sirens will be emitted so you can locate the ships in this blackness."

Immediately, sirens rang. They sounded closer than Marshall would have imagined, but not as close as he would have liked. Bonnie and he followed the sound blindly, changing directions when they had to, desperately trying to find a path through the fire and devastation.

Around them, there were people. Crowds and crowds. Doubtless people were doing as they always did, screwing, and breaking, and whatever else, though perhaps they were frightened enough to actually concentrate on saving themselves. Marshall didn't know. He couldn't see. He couldn't hear either, given all the noise. He was glad he couldn't, in a way. He could imagine they were being sane.

They found a ship. With all the other people around them, they rushed on board.

Chapter Five

The ship was chaos. People and soldiers were everywhere. Smoke too, since the doors were still open for everyone to stream in—anyone who was there. All comers. Marshall and Bonnie could still feel the shaking of the ground.

Marshall could see finally, barely. Smoke still poured in, but the ship had a gigantic fan system going, trying to suck it all back out again. The roar of the machinery was deafening. Everyone yelled at the top of their lungs whenever they needed to be heard—a madhouse.

Whether or not people had been freaked out in the blackness outside, they were calm inside the ship. Well, they were still freaking out, running around and screaming everywhere, but it was a more ordinary panic—befitting the danger and confusion of the situation. It was still an emergency, but they weren't in apocalypse mode anymore.

Presuming they had been before. Marshall didn't know.

In the middle of the mess, Marshall reflected how people lost it in some basic way every time an apocalypse happened, and then flipped once the rescue began, even if the danger was still present. It was as if they responded to the idea of conditions instead of the conditions themselves, change in concept thus being enough to change reactions, though material change had yet to occur.

Marshall also wondered about his habit of analyzing during apocalypses when he should have been focused on survival. It was a dumb trait, and he realized it. Still, he kept analyzing.

At least they were finally using the ships again, Marshall noted. Ships were such a handy thing when apocalypses were on the planet surface, and they were so rarely used—other than the one apocalypse where they fled the solar system. The flood apocalypse? Nope. The lizards? Nope. Why not?

He could understand when they didn't use them for the cosmic radiation apocalypse. There was nowhere to go in time. Except, wasn't there? They'd known about the cloud enough in advance to build the shelters. It seemed like they could have jetted everyone off for a while instead. It would have been safer. When he stopped to think about it, that didn't make sense either. Poor planning.

But, they were finally using the ships. Marshall was pleased, at least with that much. The ships were a hell of a thing to have gone through the trouble of building to be used once.

Soldiers marched around and ordered people about. Demanding names, checking lists, telling people where to go. It wasn't as nicely organized as the last flight, but the last time had been in advance of disaster instead of in the middle of it. There had been more time to plan.

Contrary to what Malcolm had made it sound like, the agency was apparently trying to get organized. Marshall understood they were simply going to crowd in and take off immediately. Though that would have been safest from a volcano avoidance perspective, he'd had some concerns.

For example, what if everyone in a city got to the same ship? Could they have all fit? Would the ship have been able to take off with so much weight?

It seemed Marshall's whole city had rushed into his ship and jammed into the corridors.

Packed together and left to their own devices could have been disastrous. People wouldn't have spread out into available space in a coherent fashion. They would have smashed together, trampled people, and overbalanced the load. Meanwhile, comfortable space could have been available right around a corner. Some order was necessary.

Marshall was glad they hadn't kept everyone choking and blind outside while they figured out who should go where. That would have been bad too, a bigger mess.

Given available choices, Marshall didn't think the Apocalypse Amelioration Agency had done too poorly. Cram everyone into the ship to get them out of the noxious, death-filled environment.

Then, once they could see and be seen, figure out where to stash them. It was a sane plan.

Of course, Marshall would have preferred if they'd taken off already. He thought of the volcanic activity and wanted to be on the ground as short a time as possible. What if an eruption caught the ship? What if ash became too thick to fly? Maybe shuffling people around would have been better handled in the air.

He admitted he didn't fully know what was going on. Maybe they knew when it was safe to take off and when wasn't. He doubted it, but he couldn't know for sure. Maybe more people needed to board. He didn't expect the ship to preserve his safety while abandoning others—that was not reasonable.

More rumbling shook the ship. People in the crowds screamed. There was apparently another reason for not taking off yet. Redistribution between ships.

Malcolm said to get inside the ships, but they weren't apparently launching that way. Maybe it had been the plan, and then maybe the load was too unequal, and plans changed. The agency might have thought people would create fewer problems if they made for any ship, and then were assisted to the right one afterward.

Marshall didn't know.

What Marshall did know was the soldiers had some kind of scheme they were following. Some people were sent to other areas of the ship. Others were told they were being taken to other ships. No one told Bonnie and Marshall anything as of yet. They were still waiting.

The corridors began to thin out. People were sent places, wherever. Marshall didn't care much. He was only observing. That's all there was to do, other than worry about volcanoes taking out the ship.

The clamor calmed more as the congestion in the corridors decreased. Fewer people made less noise. Fewer people meant less to shout over.

The air improved, Marshall noticed. That wasn't attributable to the traffic jam. Perhaps the fans were turned up higher, or everyone had finally been loaded and the doors were shut.

Again, Marshall didn't know. He only knew he could breathe better.

Finally, the soldiers got to Marshall and Bonnie. Or rather, Bo and Shelly. The hallways were pretty empty. They were the last ones to be directed.

They were shown to quarters together, big quarters in fact. It seemed like they had a whole wing of the ship to themselves. The soldier who escorted them shrugged when they mentioned it. He, or she, was merely directing people where he, or she, had been told to direct them. Again, it was hard to determine a soldier's gender, even sometimes when he, or she, spoke, particularly when breathing apparatuses were in use.

Big quarters. A palace, so to speak. All to themselves.

Marshall wondered. Though their quarters had been spacious on the trips to and from the other planet, this dwarfed by comparison. How long were they going to be in orbit? The relatively smaller rooms for the other trips had been intended for months. Was this to be longer? Perhaps permanent?

Then again, maybe that was it. The voyage before had a set duration. They might not have known precisely how long the journey would take, but they had an approximate idea. The duration was definitely finite. This however, was until the earth's surface decided to be safe again.

Maybe the agency couldn't be sure when that would happen.

Marshall was hesitant about that line of thinking. They'd been given more space on the last voyage than was in their original apartment. Block housing was a special case, so he didn't include it in the considerations. The original apartment however, had been smaller, and supposedly permanent. Quarter sizes had a strange relation to intended length of stay.

But, why, then? Why assign so much space? Marshall's mind wouldn't let the issue alone.

Perhaps the Apocalypse Amelioration Agency had been too aggressive in the shifting of people. Too many in the ship to begin with, then reworked so heavily there were too few. Or, too many assigned to other portions of the ship. That was easily possible, Marshall conceded.

Of course, perhaps there was no explanation. Maybe it'd just happened. He was likely overthinking again. Marshall admitted the possibility.

Regardless, they were alive.

"There's nobody," Bonnie exclaimed, apparently having similar thoughts. "Nobody at all."

"We didn't see many people on the last trip either," Marshall pointed out. He'd finally convinced himself to let it drop and didn't want her to get him going again.

"We didn't leave our quarters last time," Bonnie shot back. "We wouldn't have seen anyone."

This was true. Last time they hadn't known each other well and spent their time correcting that, learning each other. They hadn't left their rooms much—simply talked and whatnot with no desire to speak to anyone else, see anyone else. No chance to run across others.

Not that Marshall had left these quarters much either. He'd slept a great deal, passing time. He was waiting for an opportunity to further their plans and was sure one wasn't going to come along for a while.

Bonnie however, went walking in common hallways and corridors. She roamed and searched. Marshall didn't think she wanted to interact with anyone and she instead seemed concerned.

It was odd. Odd things bugged her.

Honestly, it bugged Marshall too. Still. He tried to force it out of his mind. There were so many odd things all the time; he'd go crazy worrying about it all. Besides, if it did mean something was there anything that could be done?

They agreed to disagree, at least on the surface.

Marshall continued to sleep. Bonnie kept roaming the ship, looking for people. She became increasingly disturbed as she explored further from their quarters without finding anyone. The ship was deserted. Her reports and increasing panic unsettled him, as much as he tried not to admit they did—to her or to himself.

He could keep himself from dwelling on the situation by not going to look for himself. As long as it was just something she said, he could rationalize she hadn't been thorough, that she hadn't covered enough ground. She'd somehow missed all the people on board. It was possible, coincidence. It would have been different if he'd gone with her and experienced the strange emptiness for himself. Eerie. That would have been harder.

That's what he couldn't understand. Why push it? What could they do about it anyway? Discovering something was going on would only make life more difficult. Until there was a possible course of action or something they could understand, it seemed best to ignore the situation.

So, Marshall slept more. Bonnie explored more. Nothing was solved, nothing moved forward. Quite a bit of time passed in this fashion. Marshall wasn't sure how much.

Bonnie ran into their quarters and screamed, "I found somebody."

"What? What's going on?" he asked groggily.

"We're not alone," she explained. "I found someone."

"Great." He rubbed his eyes. "See? I told you, nothing to worry about. You missed them before."

She shook her head. "No. Soldiers. I just saw soldiers at the end of a corridor. I shouted to them, but they were gone by the time I got there. They avoided me. They're the only ones I've found."

"I'm sure there's still citizens somewhere," he countered. "You hadn't seen the soldiers previously. There are probably still citizens you haven't found either."

"No way." She dropped onto the bed next to him. "You don't get it. I've been over the entire ship. Over and over it. There wasn't anyone."

"What about the soldiers?"

Bonnie grimaced. "I think they've been keeping out of sight. I don't think we were supposed to know they're here."

He sat up. "That's ridiculous. Even if true, it's still ridiculous. Sure there are soldiers on board, there are always soldiers—and other people too. An empty ship wouldn't make sense."

"I wish I could see the ship's manifest," she muttered, "to know for sure."

"Look it up," Marshall pointed at the terminal setup across the room. "We've got one and haven't used it. Maybe the manifest is accessible."

"Right," she scoffed, "like if something is funny they'd let me see it in the manifest." She walked over to the terminal setup anyway. It came on as she tapped at it. Her face fell. She stood looking at a screen.

"Well?"

"Found something. The manifest is the only thing I actually can access. Everything else is blocked off or endlessly tries to load without giving an error message."

He shrugged. "And?"

She turned toward him, not looking pleased. "Besides us, the ship is full, but only with soldiers. Tons of them. The ship was scheduled to be full of people when it was originally boarded, but they were all transferred. Soldiers from other ships came here. They were only ones to come here."

Marshall swallowed. His stomach ached.

"So—"

The lights went out. All of them. Every indicator, lamp, everything. The room was completely black. The doors to their quarters slid open. Marshall and Bonnie heard other doors further down slide open as well. From far off, a small light source lit up—the only light they could see.

They felt the light far off down the hall call to them. It pulled Bonnie and Marshall toward it.

They had little choice.

Chapter Six

A lone light proved to be a powerful thing. Marshall had heard how light in darkness affected animals. Some would freeze. Others, when it wasn't shone directly in their eyes, would be compelled to head toward it.

The light was not shone at Bonnie and Marshall, but it beckoned from far off down the corridors of the ship. They were being pulled.

Marshall didn't want to go. Every nerve ending in his body was screaming DANGER! At him.

He didn't say anything, as if whoever was responsible for the light could hear them, but he could tell Bonnie felt the same. She chewed a fingernail and fidgeted. At the same time, he could see she was readying her legs to walk.

Not like they had much choice. Obviously, they'd been caught. It was a trap and they'd stupidly fallen for it. The power had all been turned off except for whatever was off in the distance. They could sit in the dark for a while, stubbornly, but sooner or later they'd have to go.

There simply wasn't anything else to do.

Besides, what could get worse? They were in an enclosed box surrounded by the vacuum of space. Escape from the ship simply wasn't possible. Likely, the ship's instruments would detect where they were at any time if they tried to hide anyway. For the moment, they were allowed to delay the inevitable, but it was inevitable.

How long would even that go on? Those responsible for the light could grow impatient. Sooner or later, it could be forced.

Walk down the hall, face whatever it was.

Marshall figured they might as well get it over with. He started walking. Bonnie joined him. His fear was unawareness of where the corridor led, and what was up with all the dramatics, rather than dread of a particular punishment.

After all, surely the ship's various sections could be individually sealed. Obviously, the soldiers knew how to be in other parts of the ship. Why not section him and Bonnie off from the rest of whoever else was on board and kill the air? That would have been certain, and quick, and efficient. Why play games? That, more than anything else, other than possibly an animal-level instinct at being in the dark, is what actually bothered Marshall—the theatrics.

What kind of predator toyed with its prey when victory was certain? Some did he knew, but only out of instinct for hunting practice. Marshall knew of none who did it out of cruelty, and cruelty was the only explanation he could see. That would be odd, given the Apocalypse Amelioration Agency was usually better characterized as bureaucratic rather than cruel.

Efficiency was their underlying design, efficiency, and expediency. Neither explained the gag with the lights and the corridors.

The going was slow. Though the hall was empty, it was still dark. Bonnie and Marshall crept along to keep from stumbling. The light was far enough off it didn't help them see, though it gave them a point to move toward.

Marshall told himself that's why he was going slow.

He couldn't figure it out. Him and Bonnie had no weapons. The agency had to know. Even if they managed to make some, the two of them were no match for a single soldier. There were no tricks they could play, no way to get the drop on anyone. Neither of them had ever been in an actual fight, other than blasting a zombie or two. Soldiers were trained for combat, even if the training didn't get used much. So. . . why?

Even if the agency didn't want to risk a single soldier's life, or somehow believed Bonnie and Marshall were capable of more than they were, there was the other option Marshall had already thought of. Seal them off and kill them were they stood. No mess, nothing to fight against. No unnecessary casualties.

There wasn't a reason to take them alive, was there? Was there something they knew the agency wanted before they were dispatched? Even if so, why not simply section them off and introduce a sedative into the air supply—wait until they were knocked out to move in. Why not? The agency had that sort of thing, why not use it?

Marshall kept walking forward. There was only one place any of that would get answered . . . the end of the corridor—wherever the light was. He couldn't stop asking, but he understood wondering was useless.

Alone in the darkness.

Well, not alone. Bonnie was there with him, but worrying about her fate as well as his own made him feel more alone. Also, they had to be concerned too much with managing not to fall, hands outstretched in front of them, to be able to touch.

That was a lot like being alone together.

At one point in the darkness, Bonnie's hand reached for the wall as she stumbled forward. She screamed.

"I felt somebody."

Marshall ran over, as best he could in the dimness. They peered closely. Just barely, they could make out the form of a soldier standing motionless as a column. Then, as they got close, they could make out others standing to either side. All were in the same pose, all at attention.

"Statues," Marshall laughed. He waved his hand in front of the thing's face and got no response, no movement. "Weird. Statues."

Bonnie checked the other side of the hallway. "There's more over here. They line both sides, probably for a while now. I wonder why."

Marshall was the next one to scream. "It moved."

"What?" Bonnie asked, cringing.

"One moved. He shifted from one foot to the other."

They both backed away into the center of the hallway. They kept staring at the sides though they couldn't see the soldiers from there.

"You're crazy," she said. "It's a trick of the light, right?"

Marshall shook his head. "No . . . I'm sure. They're alive, standing still for some reason."

"Hey." Bonnie demanded, running up and pushing one before jumping back. "What gives? What do you guys want?"

None of the soldiers answered. None of them, from what Bonnie and Marshall had been able to see, moved other than to shift slightly. For whatever reason they were doing what they were doing, and they kept doing it.

"This is insane," Marshall commented.

"Seems so."

They turned and continued down the hall toward the light. Though it changed nothing, the endless line of soldiers on either side made the dark corridor even creepier—more menacing. Both he and Bonnie stayed precisely in the center.

The light was closer. They began to be able to see the soldiers lining the hall more clearly. It didn't provide any comfort. The soldiers were all dressed in identical blue battle armor, weapons ready. The line stretched ahead and behind Bonnie and Marshall, an endless number of soldiers who were surely not there when Bonnie and Marshall had started walking.

After what seemed like hours, Bonnie and Marshall could see normally. The corridor opened into a large room, the ceiling easily fifty feet high. The room was circular. Inside was a glass room structure, square with a roof about twelve feet high. Blinds were arranged on the inside of the glass structure, so Bonnie and Marshall weren't able to see inside. There was an open doorway.

The light came from within.

Soldiers also lined the walls of the large room, surrounding the glass structure. Bonnie and Marshall halted in front of the open doorway, but the soldiers still made no movement—continuing to stand at attention. Bonnie and Marshall looked at each other.

"Well?"

Bonnie shrugged, gritting her teeth. They walked in through the open door.

Malcolm sat at an immense wooden desk in the center of the room. It looked like actual wood, definitely an antique. Two plushly cushioned wood chairs sat in front of the desk, empty, but these were not quite as finely carved as the stately high-backed leather and black wood monstrosity Malcolm sat in. He wrote with a pen on a piece of paper, a stack of loose pages in a pile nearby. He was actually using old pen and paper.

"You'll both pardon me," he said, not looking up. "You took your time so I decided to get some items accomplished I've been putting off. Come in though. Come in and sit." He put the pen down, motioned at the chairs, and looked up at them.

They sat.

Malcolm looked at them. "Now, how about you two tell me what the hell you've been doing? Assume I know everything, because I do for the most part. Hijacked broadcast, lizard costumes, laxatives, missiles, protests, picnics, and so on. We've been watching for you for a while. To be honest, you seem like total lunatics."

Bonnie and Marshall looked at each other. Inside the glass structure, they didn't feel the immediate presence of the soldiers. It felt as if they'd just dropped in for a chat, perhaps for a stern lecture. Marshall didn't know how to take it.

"You're. . ." Bonnie hesitated. "You're Malcolm."

He waved a hand. "Yes, yes. In more ways than you know. Get to the point."

Marshall looked at Bonnie again. She shrugged. He supposed she was right. What did it matter? Why lie? It wasn't as if they could talk their way out of what was already known. They might as well take the opportunity to air their grievances.

"We're sick of it all," he exclaimed. "We couldn't take it anymore."

Malcolm raised an eyebrow. "Sick of it?"

"All of it. The apocalypses, one damned one after another. People getting all worked up as if it didn't happen every day, or close enough to it anyway. It's meaningless, it makes life meaningless. It's going to keep happening and happening and happening as long as there are people around for it to happen to. If there weren't, things would be different—it'd just be the way things are. That seemed better, the only better way. Stop everything," Marshall babbled. "It had to stop."

Malcolm turned to Bonnie. "This is how you felt as well?"

"Yes," she replied defiantly.

He leaned back, as much as his enormous and imposing chair would allow. "Well then," he said, "we'll have to take you out of the whole apocalypse equation. Nothing else for it, I suppose."

Bonnie shot up out of her chair. "So you're going to kill us? Just like that? You're as screwed up as any of this."

Marshall was about to calm her, get her to sit back down, but why he? Why? Let her yell. What difference would it make? At least she'd have her say first.

The clicking of readying weapons around the glass structure changed Bonnie's mind. She got quiet. It may have been easy to forget about the soldiers when they weren't visually present, but the soldiers didn't forget. Bonnie's face paled and she sat down again.

"Stand down." Malcolm called out to the soldiers. "You misunderstand me," he said to Bonnie. "I wasn't referring to an execution. Perhaps I should have been clearer. No matter how many of these we schedule, I never seem to quite get the hang of it."

"What are you talking about?" Bonnie snapped.

Malcolm pulled off his wig and laid it on the desk, the facial hair as well. He was completely bald. Even eyebrows. They'd known about the costume, but it still took them by surprise. They also hadn't expected him to be in his early thirties, that couldn't be right.

"I imagine this is easier if you look at me as me instead of as Malcolm," he said, "though that's complicated as well—since my name is actually Malcolm. I'm the only one of the Malcolms who is actually named Malcolm."

"Malcolms?"

Malcolm stared at them. The look felt different now it wasn't Malcolm doing the looking. Marshall wasn't as impressed as he had been. Well, he was but he wasn't. Marshall was about to give up on trying to sort it all out. He was getting a headache.

"You've been living in what is essentially a terrarium, an artificial environment run by the Apocalypse Amelioration Agency. The agency is run by Malcolm, or rather by Malcolms. For the purposes of the illusion we create, we become Malcolm. There's too much involved for one person, and it's been going on for too long. No one notices Malcolm never ages. It provides the only stability most people need."

"Illusion." Bonnie spat. "So it's all fake? Nobody dies? What the hell?"

Marshall had been too stunned to speak, but he thought Bonnie expressed the idea pretty aptly. What the hell? was about all Marshall could think.

Malcolm shook his head. "This isn't that simple." He rubbed his hairless brow, getting up from the desk and pacing. "Yes, some of the apocalypses are created emergencies, manufactured. Some are real problems we either allow to get out of hand or make worse. Still, others are genuine problems on their own. And no, sometimes people die. Nowhere near, even vaguely near, how many it seems, but people do die at times. We can't avoid that without destroying the illusion."

Malcolm sat down and faced them.

Marshall blinked. "What? You're willing to do this though you know some people will die? Create, let get worse, stimulate, whatever. You really do that? Even if it isn't many who die? Why?" As many impossible things as he'd had to believe, he simply couldn't swallow that one—not from such an apparently mild-mannered man.

Malcolm sighed. His body sagged. "You have to understand the psychological makeup of the average human being, what it was like before. People are instinctively afraid to live, tied to the grave from birth. They desperately need for something to stand next to, to be bigger than themselves. They desire things big enough to leave a mark on time."

He paused. Bonnie and Marshall watched, waited.

"If it isn't given to them," he said gravely, "they will create it."

Malcolm appeared to chew on his own words for a moment. It didn't feel like a time to interrupt with questions. More seemed to be coming, but Malcolm apparently needed to gird himself first.

"Before the Apocalypse Amelioration Agency," he continued finally, "no outlet existed for this impulse. It made its own outlet though. It always did. Death cults, genocide, blood sport, religious wars, mass destruction of countless different kinds. There were any number of sources, like a hydra. Cut off one head and another would inevitably grow."

"A what?"

"An antiquated reference," Malcolm muttered dismissively, waving a hand. "Forget it. It isn't important and it would mean nothing to you. What is relevant is the agency had to bring about the terrarium in order to get a handle on the situation—controlled destruction. Pressure had to be relieved before it exploded, as often as necessary. Usually, too often. This is the genius of the Apocalypse Amelioration Agency, what we actually do."

Bonnie and Marshall stared at each other. The concept was horrifying, but so was what they'd thought was going on. The facts were terrible, and the alternative was terrible. Life was horrifying.

"Yes," Malcolm agreed with the unspoken thought, "it's evil. However, for the time being, we believe it to be a necessary evil. With hope perhaps someday the terrarium can be dismantled. I look forward to that like nothing else. Until such a day arrives though . . ." He raised his palms upward, shrugging.

"So," Marshall finally said after Malcolm finished talking, "what do you mean by taking us out of the apocalypse equation then?"

"Simple." Malcolm folded his hands on the desk. "Not everyone lives in the terrarium. It exists for those who need it, but the true human society is outside. When people don't need the dollhouse anymore, we remove them—bring them into the fold. Let actual life begin."

"Another world?"

"Another world, another way of life—an actual way of life. It's been this way for a long, long time, since almost the start of the terrarium itself. We had to, if the terrarium was to be able to function. The outside is the real world. You've been living in the make believe."

"And no more apocalypses?" Bonnie asked.

The smile on Malcolm's face drew thin. "You'll have the universe as it truly is, no trumped up or exaggerated emergencies. If you let your problems get bad through neglect, you'll have to deal with the consequences. Things happen. One day, humanity will end. Life has no meaning without the threat of death, unfortunately. But, what will happen will be whatever happens. Nothing more."

Marshall had a sudden thought. "Was this what happened to the Jews? Back when they disappeared?"

"No." Marshall frowned. "We don't know what happened there, it wasn't us. Outside the terrarium, there is still a great deal that is a mystery. But, that's life." He smiled again.

Bonnie and Marshall smiled back. Everyone smiled. For once, there seemed to be something worth smiling about.

"We only ask," Malcolm went on, "you be sure you're completely ready before the transition. Look deep. Ultimately, we will let you out if you seem ready, but the internal workings of your minds are still unknown to us. Is what you find out there going to be enough?"

"Enough?"

"Life as it is. Any worth you find will be what you've found. Any meaning, the same. No one is going to give you the answers you've been looking for. There's no big reveal, other than what I've already said, at least on this side of death. The only thing we know out there is people in the terrarium don't know how to be alive. Is that going to be enough? Think carefully. What there is will be all there is."

Bonnie and Marshall looked at each other again, anxiously wondering.

"Well? What will it be?" Malcolm asked.

Chapter Seven

Marshall awoke. He was alone in bed, alone in the bedroom of the new house. It didn't appear to bother him as he rolled over. Quickly, his eyes blinked open wide. Inspiration.

"I wonder," he mumbled to no one.

He jumped out of bed. The covers slipped to the floor, he left them there. He stretched, groaning slightly.

Rubbing sleep from his eyes, he padded through a doorway into a workshop. Half-assembled machines were scattered everywhere. Instruments, chemicals, parts, the room was a mess. It wasn't that a disaster had struck. It was more like Marshall had too many projects going to keep the place tidy. It was a good mess, his mess. It was his workshop.

He got to work clearing off a table in the center. No simple task, the table was highly cluttered with an assortment of different devices. He was careful, not simply sweeping it all onto the floor. He didn't want anything broken, though he did heap it all elsewhere. He certainly didn't tidy as he cleaned.

After the table was clear, he put a large empty glass canister on the table center. It was cylindrical, clear, with high walls. Open at the top, it was sufficiently sized so he could easily have fit his head inside.

He didn't.

Instead, Marshall grabbed a worn black brick and placed it inside the container. The brick was light, some variety of polymer rather than ceramic. It made more of a click noise upon contacting the bottom of the container than a clunk sound. Marshall looked at the brick in the container for a moment. Then he grabbed a jug of liquid, unlabeled, and poured a translucent pink chemical inside. He made sure the brick was well covered, submerged.

He watched. The immersed brick was plainly visible, but nothing happened. No fizzing, no bubbles, no nothing.

Marshall seemed to expect this. He monitored the container for a while, but never frowned or wrinkled his brow. Finally, he glanced up at a nearby time screen and nodded, verifying something. Then he grabbed a kinetic rifle from a pile of junk.

Actually, it didn't appear to exactly be a kinetic rifle anymore. Modifications had obviously been made. The case was cracked open. Various components were removed, added, rerouted. The additions outweighed the subtractions so the original casing no longer fit. The modified rifle was bulkier, something different than what it had been before.

There was also an added adjustment knob on the side. Kinetic rifles didn't usually require adjustment. They shot. That's all they did.

Marshall aimed the rifle at the container. He activated it and the air in between began shimmering. Nothing moved though. The container, with the brick and the liquid inside, stayed in place. The table did as well. The shimmering continued.

This did not seem to disturb Marshall.

He fiddled with the adjustment knob. The shimmering wavered as he did so. He turned the knob slowly, in tiny increments. All the while, he kept the rifle pointed at the brick.

At one point, the container began to rattle. Not much, but visibly and audibly. Marshall quickly turned the knob back the other direction.

In the path of the shimmering, the brick began to melt. At first, it merely liquefied, slowly. Black sludge intermingled with the clear pink liquid, but didn't mix. As Marshall kept the activated rifle trained on the container, no longer adjusting the knob, the black sludge separated into red and brown goo. The clear pink liquid was absorbed. However, the red and brown goo didn't recombine with each other, remaining separate though together. The red goo drifted to the top of the container. The brown to the bottom.

The brick was gone. No more pink liquid remained either.

Marshall deactivated the kinetic rifle and set it aside. He walked over and picked up the container. He spun it around, swirling the goo inside. The liquids remained separate. He put it back on the table.

"Huh."

A clattering came from outside. He put a lid on the container and padded out, through the bedroom. It led to a living room he walked through to a patio. The sun was still in the process of rising, having peeked above the horizon.

It was not the sun. A sun. Marshall and Bonnie weren't on earth anymore. Obviously it wasn't the sun. It was not what they'd come to know of as the sun. They hadn't discussed what to know this one as yet.

Bonnie was on the patio removing gear. She had on a climate suit with several tanks on the back. She had a number of carry packs with her, tools and components. That's what the clattering had been. Some Marshall could identify and some he could not. She did different work than he did, knew things he did not.

"Desalination plant installation?" he asked.

"Yup," she replied, tossing off another carry pack. "Out in the sand parts of the lowlands. Figured it was better to go out there early. I don't get how a seaside area can get so hot while still having water, but it sure does. Maybe the salt concentration has something do with it."

Marshall nodded. He didn't think so, but he was glad she was doing what she enjoyed in any case. This time, no laxatives.

"You been up to anything yet?"

He nodded again. "Figured out how to get the synth blocks to break down to the original ingredients again. Vibrating the molecules managed to finally break the bonds."

She smiled. "The others should be excited."

Synth blocks had been bugging Marshall. They were a great building material, easily created, strong, lightweight, and durable. However, they did wear out eventually—lost their form. That would have been fine, merely make more and replace them regularly, but something had to be done with the old ones. They didn't break down and the original solvents used in their

172

construction didn't alter the finished bricks themselves. Worn out blocks piled up in refuse areas.

Not anymore though. Vibration at a particular frequency loosened the molecular bonds enough the solvents took it all back apart. They could put them together as needed, and then disassemble when they didn't. Separate out the constituent parts once more and new synth bricks could be formed from the previously used materials—a sustainable system.

It was a real solution to a real problem. Marshall liked that, actually working toward something. Progress.

Well . . . progress according to how things were defined. Marshall still didn't think there was an objective progress. In the big scheme, what made one thing better or worse than another? Nothing. What was, was. If it changed, then the change was the new what was. Six of one, half a dozen of the other. It only mattered from an individual's, or collective of individuals', perspective.

Still, this mattered from his perspective, from his and Bonnie's perspective. They had definitions and it was progress according to those.

Bonnie hugged Marshall, at least as well as she could with all those tanks on her back. They stood quietly, watching the sun continue to rise. Marshall gave her a light squeeze.

"Hard to believe, isn't it?" she asked.

"Yeah."

She smirked. "It's the end. The end of our apocalyptic world."

He looked at her. "Shut up."

Interlude

Me again, I'm sure you're thrilled.

They've been harping on it again. Thoughts. Separate identity. Maintain the distinction. Don't get confused, all that sort of thing. I wonder if they keep on the others in the same fashion. Perhaps, or perhaps I'm a special case.

After all, maybe being the only Malcolm named Malcolm carries a higher risk of blurring. I could see that, forgetting the Malcolm I am isn't the same as the Malcolm as which I perform.

Is there actually a difference? There must be, if they are so focused on me remembering it. Still, I'm not sure what danger there is in forgetting . . . or the point.

Perhaps that indicates a problem in itself.

They've gotten more specific though. The press has gone beyond merely a desire I write my own, individual thoughts. Now there is a particular instructed purpose—an assignment. There is something they want to know.

I suppose that's an improvement. At least I have an idea what they want, so I'm less paralyzed by the problem of too many possibilities, less stymied by blank pages and the silence in my head. But . . . only so much. To some extent, the specifics are as open as the lack of specifics before. I can almost no more imagine and certainly have no more ideas.

What would I do if the agency were ended?

Organizations, even temporary ones, tend to work toward the perpetuation of their own existence—keep themselves going even when their actual goal is to accomplish their own destruction. An entity, even a theoretical one formed of groups of people working under a common framework, has an instinct to survive. That which lives usually wants to continue doing so.

Results can be displeasing when it comes time to fold up shop. Purposes turn dark and warp, redefined, so it seems a point still exists. Denial. Totalitarianism. Power, control. The creation of something that turns out to be worse than the original evil whose amelioration the entity was created to work toward.

If we didn't need to create apocalypses anymore . . . what would we do? Would we politely shut our doors and go whistling on our merry way?

Or, would we keep creating them? Would we cease to let people out? Would we start to insist they weren't actually ready? Would we become an apocalypse ourselves?

I can understand the fear.

So . . . what would I do? Perhaps I would raise dachshunds.

Perhaps I could become a breeder of champion dachshunds, the funny little short-legged dogs. So many look sad, yet have ineffectual aggressive responses—like people. It's hard not to take everything as a threat when almost everything is bigger than you. Also, when even your running away is comical.

I could develop new kinds, creating variations mimicking the coloration and pattern of every other kind of dog. Dachshund versions of everything, like they were playing dress up.

Would that be possible? It seems like I remember people used to.

Surely, I would be better though. Since I'm dreaming, why not dream big? Why not dream to be the most accomplished dachshund breeder ever?

I'd have a mansion full of dachshunds. Dachshunds in the living room, dachshunds in the kitchen, dachshunds in the bathroom. The closets would be full of dachshunds, and the faucets would run hot and cold dachshunds. Dachshunds everywhere. I'd need a big place for all those dachshunds though the yard could probably still be medium-sized. I mean, how far would the little guys need to run for exercise?

It seems like a sound idea. If they ask, that's what I'll tell them I'd do, if this all ever ended.

Of course, . . . the matter wouldn't likely end there. They'd probably have follow up questions. I'm not ready for that, the whole thing would fall apart, the card house of imaginary wiener dogs. Those poor little dogs.

What suggests I'd like to do that? I've never had a dog. I've never thought about having one. Actually faced with a live dog, perhaps I'd even be afraid of it. Maybe dogs would hate me. I could be allergic, I have no real way of knowing. I certainly don't know I'd enjoy it. I've never actually considered the idea seriously, it just popped into my head.

Doubtless, some helpful person would bring up the fact dachshunds are extinct and have been for some time. No one can leave a little detail like that alone, always being so frustratingly, spitefully helpful.

Damn it. Accept my hollow gesture in the spirit in which it was intended.

No matter, I'd at least have an answer . *Like we haven't bred extinct creatures back to life using the sample matter in the genetic archives?* If we could do it for an apocalypse, surely we could spare resources to do it again when no more apocalypses were needed. What else would we be saving it all for?

No, they could make me dachshunds if they wanted to keep me occupied when it was all over. A breeding pair, or a few, and I could take things from there. That wouldn't be the hard part. They could manage if they wanted to.

The more difficult question is whether or not I'd want them to.

How would I know something like that? When has there been time to sit and contemplate the issue? To imagine what a dachshund-centered life would be like? Shouldn't I have a chance to try it? Why be so unreasonable as to demand it make sense now?

But, they would. Worse, this is still all hypothetical in my own head beyond the question they asked me to think about. But . . . still. Hypothetical dachshunds. Hypothetical pressings. Hypothetical arguments. Whatever, I know how it would go. I know what they're like.

Frankly, how could I come up with any idea not completely wild and half-baked? Does anyone seriously plan for what would happen if elves cornered the salad dressing industry? Has anyone developed sound strategies to deal with the possibility our blankets rebel and form their own sovereign nation?

No, we make serious plans for what is likely to happen, at least within our lifetimes.

Sure, people daydream once in a while about fanciful things. A bizarre thought enters our head and we examine it for a while, playing. How would we escape from a giant vat of vanilla pudding? Swimming wouldn't quite work, since it's more colloidal than liquid. It would be better to flatten out on the surface and ooze around, like on quicksand. Perhaps there would be a temptation to eat a little bit.

Is it a serious plan? No. Is it full of holes? Yes. Who cares? It's merely imaginings.

It's like the old thing with genies, at least for those who remember hearing about them. Who hasn't made plans on how to get the most out of those wishes? How to avoid wishes possibly being turned against you? No one actually thought it was going to happen, be relevant. The thoughts weren't serious. Even if it did, any possible facts would likely be so different from anything imaginable the plans would be for naught anyway. The mind was merely wandering.

Why subject it to legitimate scrutiny?

Who can imagine there being no more need for the Apocalypse Amelioration Agency? We beg for it, dream of it, but do any of us think it's going to happen someday? After having examined modern humankind? We seem no closer now than we did at the beginning—further away if anything.

If we can't even imagine it, how can we plan for such a day? I am as honestly baffled by the fact the question is earnest as I am in how to act on the question. I retreat into nonsense, as I often do, and debate the soundness of questioning itself.

It's a coping mechanism, I know.

Still . . . that's only more dancing around, isn't it? I seem to be quite good at that. There are infinite levels to evasion, and even admitting avoidance is a kind of avoidance—as is analyzing the admission of avoidance in the context of avoidance.

Hmmm. I'm becoming fairly argumentative and I'm not even talking to anyone. I wonder what I'd do if there were really another person here, one opposed.

Would it change anything?

Of course, perhaps I'm getting worked up over nothing. They might not intend to actually ask me what my plan is, merely get me to think. They haven't told me there would be a test. It's possible they know what sort of thing I'd hand back and wouldn't dare to ask.

I know I wouldn't.

Still . . . they might. If they did, it would probably be best not to go with the dachshunds.

I'll tell them I'd retire to the desert and become a yogurt farmer. I'd live in a mud yurt, wear robes sewn out of animal hides. Each day, before the sun became too hot, I'd walk my fields and bury activated cultures. Moisture from the air would catalyze the dirt and fresh yogurt would come bubbling up from the cracks.

The finest yogurt.

I'd collect the raw glop in clay jars using wooden implements. I'd strain it through cheesecloth, filtering out impurities and lumps. I'd let my yogurt cure by the light of the full moon, congealing and taking on special properties. Then I'd package it in bladders formed from animal organs, perhaps those of a sheep. I'd feed the world, nourishing souls as well as bodies. My yogurt would be in demand everywhere.

No flavors, no fruit. I would refuse to adulterate the purity of my yogurt. Yogurt is yogurt is yogurt, and its subtle richness would be enough.

That'd freak them right out. I ought to say it.

Would they think I'd lost my final grip? That I actually imagined yogurt was grown in the ground?

It's hard to say, they can be quite a literal bunch. I'm sure half of them are convinced I'm already crazy.

No, maybe that story isn't a good idea. I'm not cruel.

Perhaps I'll tell them I was going to learn the language of grasshoppers, live among them and conduct myself by the grasshopper laws until I was accepted as one of their own. Then, when I was a full grasshopper adoptee, I'd take a grasshopper bride—perhaps the daughter of the grasshopper king. Only then would they reveal to me the grasshopper secrets and allow me to worship their gods by dancing at the great leaf feast under the autumnal moon.

Or, I could be a dental tool salesman. . . .

ABOUT THE AUTHOR

David S. Atkinson's writing appears in *Bartleby Snopes*, *Grey Sparrow Journal*, *Atticus Review*, and other journals.

Other books by David S. Atkinson:

Not Quite So Stories

Bones Buried in the Dirt

The Garden of Good and Evil Pancakes

He spends his non-literary time working as a patent attorney in Denver.

davidsatkinsonwriting.com

CPSIA information can be obtained
at www.ICGtesting.com
Printed in the USA
LVOW10s1619190417
531397LV00009B/953/P

9 781942 856078